TAMMY CAMPBELL BROOKS

Brilliant Daye

BOOK 1

Brilliant Daye
Book 1

Author: Tammy Campbell Brooks
Title: Brilliant Daye
Book 1
Subject: fiction
African American
Publishing 2021
Paradeyez Books Publishing
ISBN-13:
978-1732276871
Library of Congress Control Number: 2021907037

Table of Contents

Books by Tammy Campbell Brooks:
The Ghetto Blues
Daddy Issues
Unapologetic Poetic
Tar Baby
Tar Baby 2 "Tianna's Story"

Brilliant Daye

Is dedicated to my family, the Campbells

Chapter One

Wednesday couldn't get here fast enough for Billy as his alarm clock sang "Could It Be I'm Falling In Love." He didn't bother to hit the snooze button like he would any other morning. Today was a special day. He'd met with Coach Walker on Monday and was informed that he would not play in this week's football game if he didn't increase his algebra grade to at least 70 percent. But he wasn't happy about not playing in the game; he was elated because he set an appointment after practice to be tutored by Sasha West, the sexiest cheerleader that he had ever laid eyes on. Billy had been trying to get close to Sasha ever since she transferred to Fox Tech High School last year, with no luck. Today, she had no choice but to look into his big brown eyes as they twinkled in the moonlight, and his tall, muscular body with oversized hands that screamed quarterback. He was ready to teach Sasha the X's and O's, but not in football.

A knock at the door jarred Billy out of his reverie. It was his little sister Brandy asking for a ride to school since her best friend who she usually rode with was sick. Billy answered through his bedroom door without inviting her in. He would be ready in twenty minutes. He needed the extra time to look nice for Sasha.

Billy and Brandy were being raised by their mother Melody, who worked two jobs to fill the emptiness of their loss. Her husband died last year in a car accident and it was a struggle emotionally for the Daye family. Billy Sr. had been coming home from Memphis, Tennessee visiting family when a drunk driver fell asleep at the wheel and drove head-on into his Ford F-150 truck. The teenage driver was convicted of manslaughter and was serving ten years in prison. His conviction could be cut in half with good behavior. His sentence was light and he was not punished to the full extent of the law because it was Billy Junior's childhood best friend, Joshua, who had been behind the wheel. Melody forgave Joshua and begged the judge for mercy, but Billy hadn't and never would as long as he lived. In fact, he prayed that Joshua never got out of prison for what he did to him and his family. He had often scolded Joshua about drinking and driving, but it fell on deaf ears. Joshua's father, James, was an alcoholic too, who often abused him and his mother.

Joshua had spent many nights at the Daye's home trying to escape the abuse of his father and even begged his mother to leave him, but she wouldn't. She didn't believe in divorce and was submissive to her husband. She often prayed that Jesus would change his heart, but he hadn't after twenty years of marriage. He seemed to get worse by the day. Every day Billy drove to school, he saw James at the bus stop, reeking of Jack Daniels, wearing clothes that hadn't been washed in weeks. Billy hated to see him in that state, but there was nothing he could do.

Brandy and Billy were a block away from school when his cell phone distracted him from James. It was Billy's best friend, Wilt, Wilt's baritone voice came through his cell phone.

"Yo, Billy, what's up with Matt telling me about you not playing in the game on Saturday?"

"It's not a rumor if it's true. I'm almost at school. I'll talk to you when I get there. One."

Billy quickly ended the call before Wilt could say anything else about *his* business. Immediately, Brandy started asking questions about his availability, and how she and Olivia were going to be at the game, and what did he mean that he's not playing?

"I have tutoring after school. I need to get my algebra grade up. I'm not worried about it," he said with a smile.

"Why are you smiling? Aren't you upset?"

"Naw, not really. I'm good and I will play in the game."

"You better. My reputation can't be tainted because of my *dumb* brother."

"Who you calling dumb?"

"You. You're the one that needs tutoring."

"I should have let you walk to school to see how dumb I am."

Billy parked in student parking and killed the engine. Brandy unlocked her seat belt and exited the car without a "thank you" or "have a nice day." She bumped into Wilt as he ran up to the car to open her door. He wanted to prove that chivalry wasn't dead.

"Hey, what are you doing?"

"Nothing. I just wanted to be a gentleman and open your door."

"Thanks, but I'm capable of opening my own door."

"Excuse me, Miss Independent Lady."

"That's right, and don't you forget it." She winked her eye, sashayed her hips, and headed for class.

Wilt watched in admiration, but that's all he could do because if Billy knew he had a crush on his little sister, Wilt would be in the hospital fighting for his life.

Billy greeted Wilt with a brotherly handshake specifically for him. Each of his friends had a secret handshake that drew onlookers' attention each time they saw each other. People didn't understand how they could remember each technique.

"So, what's up with you not playing, and why the hell you ain't mad?" Wilt asked.

"I have tutoring after school with Sasha West"

"You're lying. She doesn't tutor football players because she thinks of us all as dumb jocks."

"I know," Billy said while rubbing his hands together and stroking his neatly-trimmed mustache.

Billy admitted that he would miss any game to get an opportunity to be next to Sasha. Football was a sport, but Sasha, she was "wifey material," he joked. Wilt reminded him how he had said the *same* thing about his last failed relationship with Lisa. Lisa and Billy dated for three years before she got pregnant by her side-guy and dropped out of high school in her senior year. She had married the side-guy and had two kids. Billy should have never dated an "older" woman as a freshman in high school. She was a senior and wanted materialistic things that Billy couldn't afford to give her. After Lisa, his heart hadn't been the same—*until* he saw Sasha. Her natural curly hair and chestnut skin figuratively touch him each time he heard her cheer from the crowd. He swore she was his personal cheer team. He went to sleep and woke up thinking about her. She was intelligent, and a great tutor, or so he heard. Today, he was about to find out.

"You just had to bring up Lisa, huh? Do I ever bring up bucktoothed Rita? Do I ever throw her up in your face?"

"Her teeth weren't bucked; it was her braces. Besides, she wasn't my girl."

"Who are you trying to convince, me or you?"

"Both," Wilt joked.

They did their secret handshake and departed, going their separate ways until algebra class. Wilt sat next to Billy as Sasha walked into class talking to her friend, Laura. Wilt nudged Billy as he shook his head with a big Kool-Aid smile. Sasha acknowledged Billy with a smile of her own, and he couldn't believe it. He wanted to go to the nurse's office and borrow her stethoscope to check his heart rate. It beat like an African drum. He began to perspire, and Wilt asked him if he was okay. He excused himself to go and get a drink of water to pull himself together. He walked out just in time and returned before the tardy bell rang.

Mrs. Wilson, the math teacher, talked about the quadratic equation and how best to solve it without doing all the extra steps, but inferred that some of them may need to do it the long way and that was okay. She looked directly at Billy and the class chuckled. He smirked like "whatever." He turned to Sasha and immediately focused on her plump lips. Her lips gloss matched her outfit and aura perfectly. She smiled and winked, and he smiled back. He couldn't wait until her tutoring session.

Mrs. Wilson announced a pop quiz for the next day and instructed them to pay close attention to section twenty, on page twenty-eight. The exam would be next Wednesday, a week away. The teacher drew her attention to Billy. "Billy Daye, did you get that?" He didn't answer; he was temporarily in a trance and Sasha's lips were all that he cared about. He couldn't wait to feel them upon his. His elbow rested on his closed math book and drool was about to escape his mouth. Wilt whispered and tried to warn him that the teacher was coming. She walked to Billy's desk and asked if he was listening. He didn't hear a word she said until she took his math book from under his elbow, opened it, and closed it to make a loud sound that vibrated loudly like the ceiling was about to fall. It wasn't until then that he came back to earth and found that he was the center of the class's attention as they laughed. Mrs. Wilson asked him to stay after class. He reluctantly agreed. He had no choice.

The bell rang and Billy was the first to stand and try to exit the classroom, despite knowing he was supposed to stay.

"Not so fast, Mr. Daye," Mrs. Wilson said as she snapped her fingers. Billy hated when she did this, and she did it often. Everyone passed him on their way out the door. Mrs. Wilson asked Billy to close the door, and he did so after Wilt left, giving him a brotherly handshake. He watched Sasha wave bye. He wanted to say *see you in tutoring* but he couldn't get it out in time because Mrs. Wilson cleared her throat, distracting his attention away from her. Billy walked to her desk and she told him to have a seat next to her. She looked him in the eye and asked him what his plans were after high school. He said he was going to play pro football. She wanted to know *what else,* and he didn't quite understand what she meant. He reiterated that he was going to play pro football and make a lot of money.

"What happens if you don't make it to the NFL, or have a major injury that stops you from playing professional sports?"

"Aww. Come on, Mrs. Wilson, don't jinx me like that. You're supposed to support me."

"I am. Why do you think I'm tough on you? I've seen too many of our young men think that sports are the only way to make a lot of money, not realizing that their intelligence was a more logical path.

Billy heard her, but he was thinking in his mind that he already had a mother, and she wasn't his mom. He didn't say it out loud of respect for her. He appreciated her advice, but now was not the time. He was trying to get to practice so he could begin his tutoring session with *Sasha*. He looked outside the classroom and noticed the sky was cloudy and dark, so he changed the subject to the weather.

"It looks like it's about to rain," Billy said, pointing to the sky and asking to be excused.

Mrs. Wilson let out a sigh because she wanted the best for him and saw his potential. She also remembered the dark days when his father passed last year. She'd found him in the hallway beneath the stairs, staring into space, holding a pair of scissors in his hand. His face had been filled with sadness. She counseled him that day and felt great remorse and empathy. She knew how it felt to lose a father. She had lost hers when she was a child, to drug addiction. He was a great athlete like Billy, but had been injured and given Vicodin for the pain. He became addicted and it went downhill for her family from then on. He shot and killed himself on her older brother's birthday; a day she would never forget. Her brother had to take counseling for years due to the traumatic death of their father. She didn't want to see Billy in the same predicament.

"Well, I guess you better get going. I don't want you to be late for practice."

"Thanks for caring, Mrs. Wilson. I appreciate it."

"Anytime, Billy. Anytime," she said as she gave him a reassuring pat on the shoulder and wished him luck.

He got up from the chair and began walking toward the door. Mrs. Wilson watched as Billy turned and said, "You know, Mrs. Wilson, we need more teachers like you. You don't get paid much, but you still care about your students. Once I make it rich, I'm going to come back and hook you up. I promise."

She smiled and said, "I'm going to hold you to that. Now get out of here before I hear from Coach Walker about you being late." Billy winked at her and began jogging to practice. As soon as he reached the gym, rain began to fall. He thought practice would be canceled but no such luck. The coach was in his office waiting for his players to suit up. Rain, snow, or shine, there would be practice. The Buffaloes were 5-0 and the coach wanted the championship this year because his job depended on it.

Billy sat in front of his locker when the coach came out of his office and asked to speak to him for a second. Billy thought to himself: *what now, not another lecture. First Mrs. Wilson and now Coach, again. They're killing my vibe. I need to be in a good mood when I meet Sasha.*

"What did you do now?" Matt laughed as he saw Billy walk into the coach's office.

Billy could have socked Matt in the mouth, but he didn't want to get cut from the team. He'd already had a run-in with Matt and been suspended. Matt was an average bench warmer, so he had nothing to lose, unlike Billy. Matt was the paparazzi of the locker room. He was always in somebody's business. Billy gave him the birdie and kept walking.

"Ooh, you wish you could," Matt said as he flapped his hand in a girly gesture.

Billy hit the wall pretending like it was Matt's face.

"Ouch, that must have hurt." Matt exclaimed, laughing hard like he was watching Dave Chappelle's comedy show.

Coach warned Matt that if he wanted to play in the game, he needed to cool it. That gave Billy something to smile about because he always thought of him as a wasted roster spot on the team.

Coach closed the door to his office and told Billy to have a seat. Billy adjusted his shoulder pads before he sat down. He wanted to know what he'd done this time.

"It's nothing bad, it's just that I've been going over videos and I think it's best that—"
A knock on the coach's door interrupted the conversation. It was the assistant coach, Mr. Reed, concerned about the weather. Possible hail and thunderstorms were headed their way within the hour, and he thought that they should cancel practice for today. Reed showed the coach the local weather app on his phone. The coach read all the alerts and decided that it was in the team's best interest to cancel practice but extend it for the next day.

Billy almost jumped out of his seat when he heard the coach was going to *cancel* practice.

"All right. Let the guys know that we will add a half-hour to tomorrow's practice."

"Yes sir," Coach Reed said as he exited the office.

Billy could hardly contain himself knowing that practice was canceled. It gave him *extra* time to get ready for Sasha.

"Billy, can you stay a little bit? I want to continue what we started."

"Coach, I can't. I have tutoring today."

"That's right. That's right." Coach repeated, holding his hands up in unison as he often did when he was worried. Billy assured him that he had Saturday's game and to stop worrying so much. *He* should be the one concerned because he had to bring up his grade before the game. Billy gave the coach some dap and left to change out of his uniform and get ready for his tutoring session.

Thunder continued to roar and heavy raindrops crashed into every window that was open and not shielded. Custodians hurried to secure and close them. Billy scurried to the showers humming, "Could it be I'm falling in love with you, Sasha." He changed the lyrics of The Spinners' hit song to fit his mood and mentality. He had been falling for Sasha, and in about twenty minutes, Billy and his intoxicating Kenneth Cole cologne would finally be up close and personal with the girl of his dreams.

Chapter Two

Billy arrived early at the study hall, signed in, and took a seat waiting for Sasha. He looked around and saw there was only one tutor in session. He surveyed the room, noticed the triptych décor, and thought how creative it was. He became bored, took out his phone, and silenced it while he played a game of Tetris. He checked the time every five minutes, forgetting that he was ahead of schedule and it wasn't that Sasha was late. While distracted by his phone, a sweet whisper caught his attention. He looked up, and there stood a five-foot-nine young lady with natural hair, mahogany blemished skin, and bifocal glasses asking if he was Billy Daye. She held out her hand to greet him, introduced herself as Barbara Knight, and said that she would be substituting for Sasha who had an emergency at home and had to leave.

Billy cleared his throat and became inert as he watched Barbara's outstretched hand. He couldn't believe it. He'd waited all this time and now there was no Sasha.

"You don't want my hand to fall off, do you?" she asked.

"Oh, I'm sorry. I was just expecting…" He couldn't get the words out, so Barbara assisted him.

"Yeah, I know you were here to see my cousin, Sasha."

"Um, yeah," he said as he softly shook her hand and thought, *did she just say, cousin*?

"Oh, don't worry, you're in good hands with me. I know math like the back of my hand."
He didn't know if she was bragging or serious.

"So, you're the maven for today, huh?" he arrogantly asked.

She explained that she was no expert, but she loved math and enjoyed teaching it. She gave a brief history on how long she had tutored, and the success rate of her students passing their courses. How she had never made a "B" in any of her classes. She had a 4.0 GPA.

He seemed uninterested and watched her mouth go in and out of adagio. She was a kind young lady, and he tried his best to stay focused and show tact, but his disappointment was written all over his face. He was ready to run out of there like his ass was on fire. But he had to stay, and needed to, so that he could get his grade up. He knew neither Coach nor Mrs. Wilson was going to let him slide.

Barbara went on and on about her epoch as a tutor. She must have begun her time in history when she was first born. But he tuned her out and eventually she tapped his hand and asked if he was ready. He stood at attention as they walked to one of the rooms and closed the door. She erased the whiteboard and they both took a seat at a round table next to each other. He hadn't noticed her braces. But her teeth were straight and didn't look like she needed them. She had a cute smile too and a dimple on her left cheek. After surveying her attire, he settled down a bit and advised her that he had a quiz the next day on section twenty, page twenty-eight of his math book. He took the book out of his backpack and turned to the section and page. Barbara looked at the book and began to explain. She spoke in a manner that made him feel like he needed a dictionary to understand her. He didn't know if she was trying to *prove* to him that she was fully qualified to teach, or highly intelligent, or both. He took in every word she said and mentally wrote them down so that Webster could be his friend that night when he got home. She stood at the whiteboard and made algebra "breviloquent" as she said. *Breviloquent? What the hell does that mean?* he thought. He didn't ask. He went along with the flow and mentally filed the word for his homework assignment with the dictionary. The strange part about the tutoring session was that she simplified the quadratic equation and the light bulb in his head was on high beams. He began to *get it*. Billy was beginning to understand algebra.

The forty-five-minute tutoring session ended too quickly, and Billy wanted to stay longer. Barbara gave him math problems to solve, and he did them with ease and couldn't wait for each one. She gave him homework too. He thanked her and said that he *thought* he got it. She assured him that if he used the methods she taught him, he would be fine. He made another appointment for reassurance, but hopefully, Sasha would be back. He felt that he owed Barbara an apology after the way he came at her in the beginning, nonchalant and arrogant.

"Yo, Barbara, I want to apologize for how I doubted you. I didn't think you were good enough to teach someone like me."

"No, there's no need to apologize. I am used to being treated that way, and besides, everyone signs up to be taught by Sasha." She continued packing books in her book bag as she said this.

"Do you need a ride home or anything? You know, the weather is bad out there."

She thought twice about accepting a ride because she really didn't know Billy; she only knew of him. They didn't run in the same circles and this year was her first at Fox Tech. She had been in a private school, but her father lost his job because of the heartbreak of his wife leaving him for a man almost half his age. He had found another one soon after and It had been her father Leon and her, ever since Barbara was ten years old. She was an only child and daddy's little girl. She was spoiled rotten to the core, but you couldn't tell by the way she carried herself. She was confident, intelligent, awkward, but in a good way. She was unique.

"Yes, sure. But umm, you're not... Ummm. How do I say this...?"

"Say what? I'm not what?"

"You're not one of those Jeffrey Dahmer's, right? A serial killer? I mean, my dad won't find my head in a refrigerator?"

"Girl, what? Naw, I left my chainsaw at home, so you're going to be aiight for the day." He laughed as he threw his book bag over his shoulder and offered to carry Barbara's as they exited the study room and headed toward student parking to retrieve his car. She giggled but refused his generosity because she had her Mace in her book bag ready to aim if anything were to go down. She opened her umbrella as she texted her father to let him know that she was on her way home and that she was getting a ride from a student, BILLY DAYE. She capitalized his name. Leon responded OKAY and that he was working late and would pick up dinner. He asked what she wanted, and she replied Lucino's veggie pizza. Her father smiled. He knew exactly what she wanted because she always wanted Lucino's pizza. They ended the text with: "Love you, more."

Billy opened the passenger door for Barbara as she folded her umbrella and got inside. She tried to shield him from the rain, but he refused because he was a man's man and never carried an umbrella. His Dallas Cowboys hat was good enough. He and his father drove each year to watch the Cowboys play on Thanksgiving Day. A tradition since Billy was five years old.

He sprinted to his side of the car, got inside and reached into the back seat of the car to acquire a towel he always kept nearby. He offered it to Barbara, and she accepted it, wiping the rain from her arms. She took her glasses off and began to clean them. Billy glanced at her and thought, *she isn't bad looking without her glasses but she's no Sasha.* He let the relationship connection sink in. *She's Sasha's cousin.*

"So, are you hungry? he asked to break the silence as he turned on the radio.

"My dad is bringing home veggie pizza. I'm good."

"Are you a veterinarian? I mean, you don't eat meat?"

"No, I'm a *vegetarian* and I don't eat meat." She chuckled.

"Yeah, that's what I meant, *vegetarian*. He felt like an airhead, but she corrected him without being patronizing.

He wanted to ask why she didn't eat meat but didn't want to get too personal. She offered anyway as if she'd read his mind. She talked about the environment and how animals are treated before they are killed, and how she watched a documentary on animals being slaughtered and abused so that humans could eat beef. She decided that she could save them by refusing to eat meat. She'd held strong to her belief ever since she was seven years old.

"Makes sense. I can see you saving the world from itself," he said, flinging his arms out like he was gathering the whole world in his hands.

"I'm not going to save the world, but I will do my part in trying to make it a better place. And can you please keep *both* of your hands on the steering wheel?"

He obliged as he asked for directions to her home since she didn't want to go out for food. She gave him the route and they arrived in front of her house within ten minutes. Her home was nicely manicured and the only lights that were on came from some LED yard lights.

"You sure you don't need me to walk you to your door to make sure Dahmer isn't inside? Because I don't want your dad to find your head in the refrigerator."

She hit him slightly and they both laughed.

"Thank you so much for the ride."

"Oh, no problem. You sure you don't need me to walk you in?"

"No, Billy."

"Have a good night and don't let the bed bugs bite." He smiled and winked at her as he hopped out of the car to open her door.

"Goodnight," she whispered.

He closed the door, got back into his car, and sat there until she was inside, and he saw the porch and floodlights come on. Then he drove off into the night.

He arrived home within fifteen minutes. Placing his key into the lock and opening the door, he noticed his mom asleep in a La-Z-Boy recliner chair with her shoes off and *The Autobiography of Malcom X* resting on her lap. He gently took the book from her lap and set it on the coffee table. He turned off the lamp, went to the closet to place a blanket across her body, and kissed her forehead. He went into the kitchen to heat up the meal that his mom left in the microwave. He took the stairs two at a time to check on his sister before entering his room. He saw her in deep conversation on the phone as she threw a pillow at him to close her bedroom door. The pillow missed and fell to the floor.
He headed toward his room, turned the light on, and thought about how he needed to seriously clean it this weekend. He turned on the TV and began to watch the local news. Another unarmed Black man killed with his five-year-old daughter in the back seat of the car. He immediately changed the channel. He was immune to the violence against Black people in the hood. He wanted to eat his dinner in peace and clear his mind for the algebra quiz tomorrow morning.

He thought about Barbara and the impact her first tutoring session had on him. He would put the strategies she taught to good use and didn't want to disappoint her by failing.

His cell phone rang, and it was Wilt. Billy pressed reject but he called back. Billy thought about pushing reject call again but decided to answer after the third ring.

"Yeah, what up?"

"Hey, what up B, how did your tutoring go with *Sasha*?"

"Man, she didn't even show up."

"I told your ass. I told you, boy, that she doesn't tutor jocks. Didn't I tell you?" Wilt cuffed his fist closed and laughed into his hand.

"I signed up tomorrow for another session, so we will see." Billy hoped.

"Man, I bet you five dollars she doesn't show up."

"You owe me too much money already and I don't want you to have to give up your firstborn to pay your debt."

"Whatever, bet?"

"Later, Wilt." Billy ended the call as he set his finished plate aside and headed to take his shower. Thirty minutes later, he sat at his desk reviewing the math homework that Barbara assigned him. He finished the math problems and sat on his bed. He thought back on the conversation between him and Barbara and wished he had her number so he could pretend he was Jeffrey Dahmer. He smiled at the thought as he drifted to sleep.

Chapter Three

Barbara sat at the breakfast table enjoying her toasted bagel topped with Philadelphia cream cheese. She stood and walked to the refrigerator to pour herself a glass of orange juice. She sat back down at the table and began reading the morning newspaper. Her dad, Leon, walked into the kitchen stretching and yawning from a late-night at the office. He bent down and gave Barbara a kiss on her forehead asking her about *Billy Daye*.

"Dad, he's nobody. He's just a jock who I tutored in algebra." She smiled behind the newspaper, not knowing her father mentioned Billy to see her reaction.

"Umm hum, a jock? Is that what you're calling athletes these days? I couldn't tell he was a *nobody* by the way you capitalized his name in the text message. And I see you're wearing makeup today," he said as he gently stroked her face.

Barbara rolled her eyes and took another bite of her bagel. She changed the subject by asking her father if he wanted breakfast. He complimented her beauty, even though he preferred her natural, but it wasn't his decision. He declined her offer because he didn't want to be late for an important meeting involving a possible promotion. He was distracted by an unfamiliar text message notification from a phone number he didn't recognize. He flipped open his phone and his smile turned into a look of concern as he read:

Message: I want to see Barbara. You can't keep her from me forever. She will be eighteen next month. She has to know the truth.

He texted back immediately as he walked toward the front door.

Leon: Who is this?
Message: J
Leon: J who?
Message: JW

Before Leon could respond, he heard Barbara calling and asking if everything was all right. She came from behind to give him a hug and wished him a good day. The look on his face appeared as if he saw Casper the not-so-friendly ghost.

"What's wrong, Dad?"

"Nothing, Pumpkin, it's just work-related stuff that's all. I will see you later tonight."

"You're working late *again*?"

"Yeah, unfortunately, but I'm going to make it up to you this weekend. We can go catch a movie. And you can bring *Billy Daye* along if you want to."

He grabbed his car keys from the key hanger. Even though it was too early to admit it, her stomach caught butterflies hearing his name. She pretended she was in control of her giddiness over Billy. She had only met him yesterday when he signed up to be tutored by *Sasha*. But Billy Daye had piqued Barbara Knight's interest. She knew it and so did her father.

"Dad. Have a good day." She smiled and kissed him good-bye. She closed the front door after he drove off.

She leaned back against the door thinking about Billy. Her subconscious, being a playa hater, spoke to her: *girl, he ain't studying you, he came to see your cousin.* She snapped back to reality and responded: *you're right.* As if she was talking to someone other than herself.

She got her head out of the clouds and cleaned her breakfast area in fifteen minutes before the school bus arrived. She checked her makeup in the mirror, flossed and brushed her teeth. She retrieved her book bag, scurried to lock the front door, and walked to her designated bus stop. She saw the bus coming, and her nemesis, Kurt.

"Well, hello there, lovely lady. You're looking gorgeous as ever. You look like a buttermilk biscuit with syrup and I'm ready to slop you up."

"Mmm hmmm, those syrup lips of yours have been around too many buttermilk biscuits." Exclaimed Barbara.

"Hold up there, now, you're breaking my heart. I'm a one-woman man. Don't ever believe the hype and these chicken heads running around in the hood." He tried to plead against his Mack Daddy card.

"I thought you said you had a car anyway. Why are you still catching the bus, getting on my nerves?"

"Getting on your nerves? Look, you're too young to have nerves." His laugh sounded like he was gargling with mouthwash. "My car is in the shop getting a makeover."

"Makeover? For *two* months? It must look like Freddy."

"Freddy who?" he asked as he leaned his head to the side, closer to her lips, waiting for her response.

The bus pulled to the stop and the driver opened the door. Students from the neighborhood entered, then Barbara, followed by Kurt. Barbara sat in a seat next to a girl named Samantha. She greeted her as Kurt sat in a seat directly in back of them. He tapped her shoulder and asked again.

"Freddy who?"

She turned around to face him and said, "Krueger."

Samantha couldn't help but overhear the conversation and she and Barbara laughed out loud. Kurt sucked his teeth, sat back in his seat, and didn't say another word until they got to school.

The bus arrived and the students exited. Barbara noticed Billy Daye driving up with a girl in the front seat. She had never seen her before. It didn't look as though they were romantically involved because he didn't open her car door. The body language between them appeared nothing more than friends or maybe a relative? She pondered.

Kurt ran to catch up to Barbara, asking her to go out with him that weekend.

"How are you going to pick me up, on your bicycle?"

"Naw, I'mma have my car out of the shop by Friday."

"Whatever." She continued to walk, trying to ignore him and his advances.

"Come on girl, stop playing hard to get. Give a brother a once-in-a-lifetime chance."

"I tell you what. If you get your car out of the shop by Friday, I will go on a date with you."

"It's a date. I'll pick you up Friday at seven p.m."

"Yeah, and don't be late."

"I'll bet your grandma's undies I won't be."

"Bye, Kurt." She laughed.

She had to admit that Kurt made her laugh. His demeanor and appearance reminded her of Chris Tucker with a Jheri curl and a gold tooth. Except Kurt's curls were natural no chemicals.

Leon arrived to work before any of the other employees. He had been working in the technology field for five years. He believed wholeheartedly if you are on time, then you are late. So each morning he arrived at least thirty minutes before his scheduled shift. He walked into his office, turned on the light, and noticed the space was a mess. He had been going over documents for weeks trying to get this big promotion. The Banner software launch was near, and he was responsible. He was scheduled to meet with an Ellucian Software representative to make sure he and his staff were ready.

As he set his briefcase on the floor next to his desk and sat down in his chair, his phone beeped with a new text notification. He gasped in frustration because his mind needed to be clear before the meeting. He flipped open the phone and saw a notification from Navy Federal Credit Union alerting him that a deposit had been made to his checking account. He read the message in relief and placed his phone back on his desk. He opened his drawer and began filing some of the documents to clean up his office before the representative arrived.

Fifteen minutes later, after he'd organized his office clutter, he walked down the hallway to the breakroom to make fresh coffee. He grabbed a leftover donut and placed it in his mouth, but as he turned, in walked the promiscuous Amber Smith, gazing at him. Her mouth was within inches of his and the donut, and he could smell her minty warm morning breath. He almost choked on his donut because he wasn't expecting anyone to be there at that time. And besides, he didn't hear her enter the room. She was nicely attired in her mini dress and stilettos, her perfume was intoxicating, and as much as Leon hated her flirtatious ways, it was hard not to be sexually attracted to her. Amber pursued Leon like a moth to a flame and he had resisted for over a year. He never mixed business with pleasure, or pleasure with business, because he didn't want to get burned by the flames. Not after what happened with his ex-wife. In fact, he hadn't been in another serious relationship in eight years, and he preferred to keep it that way.

"Good morning, Mr. Knight," Amber purred.

"Top of the morning to you, Amber," he said after taking the donut from his mouth.

"Is it enough for me?"

"There's plenty." Leon pointed to the counter in the direction of the microwave where the donuts were in a box.

"I was talking about right here." She took the donut from his hand, bit it, and gave it back to him. She began licking her fingers slowly and making an *Mmmmm* sound. "It sure is good."

Leon cleared his throat and excused himself. He poured his cup of coffee and immediately left the breakroom before *oh boy* woody awakened. Amber smiled and watched Leon scurry out of the room. She loved seeing him blush, and the more he played hard to get, the more turned on she became.

"Have a good day, Mr. Knight," she yelled down the hallway.

"You too, Amber." He turned slightly, fidgeting and trying not to drop his coffee.

He entered his office and immediately closed and locked the door. He wasn't afraid of Amber, but she was the granddaughter of one of the owners of the department and Leon didn't want to bend or break any rules, especially with a promotion on the line.

The moment he sat down in his office chair, another alert broadcasted from his phone, scaring the living daylights out of him. He didn't know if it was the meeting, Amber Smith, or the earlier text message he received about his daughter Barbara that had his nerves riled up. His phone rang and he picked up after the first ring.

"Hello," Leon said.

He could only hear faint breathing and a television playing in the background.

"I'm coming for my daughter. It's been almost eight years and she's nearly eighteen. I'm coming for her, you hear me."

"Don't call me ever again or else I will have you arrested." Leon disconnected the call, scrolled down on his phone, and clicked "block caller." His heartbeat was running a race that he wanted no part of. He was unprepared, but he had always known that this day would come.

Chapter Four

Billy entered the locker room and you could hear a pin drop. It looked and felt like someone had died. He noticed the coach's office was dark, which was peculiar because Coach Walker lived in his office watching old videos and going over the playbook. To see the door closed and lights off rang, **Code 9**.

Billy walked up to Wilt and asked him what was going on. Wilt shook his head and told Billy that he didn't want to know.

"Yeah, I do, that's why I asked. Where is the coach?"

"All right everybody, can I have your attention? Line up right here guys," Coach Reed said.

The team slowly began walking to the designated area. He asked everybody to kneel. They did as they were told and the announcement was surreal, not only to the team, but especially to Billy. It was like hearing about his father's death all over again. Coach Walker was rushed to the emergency room last night for heart pains; he'd had a heart attack and was in stable condition. He would be out for a few weeks until he was able to return, and Reed was the interim.

"Is he all right? Can we go see him?" Matt asked in a trembling voice.

"Not until the family approves visitors, but I will keep you all updated on his prognosis. I know you guys mean well and are concerned, but we must leave Coach Walker's health in the Lord's hands. There's nothing any of us can do right now, but let's do him proud by winning Saturday's game."

Coach Reed was right in a sense, but Coach Walker meant more to Billy than football. Billy wanted to say, "*forget football.*" but he knew Coach Walker's character, and he would want it to be less about him and more about the team. He let every word that Coach Reed uttered sink in, asked to say a prayer for the coach and his family, and then said, "Let's kick some ass for Coach Walker."

The team cheered in agreement and didn't complain about the extra thirty minutes of practice from yesterday's canceled activities.

After practice, Billy met up with Wilt and talked a little about Coach, but mostly about his tutoring session with Sasha. Wilt guaranteed that she would be a no show again, but Billy had hope and faith that she would be there. And when he entered the study room after practice, there she stood wrapping up her tutoring session with another student. Billy smiled but also felt a sense of relief. His ego couldn't bear another letdown. He sat at the table and pulled out his cell phone to wait until Sasha was ready for him, but then he noticed Barbara. She looked amazing, more appealing than she did the day before, with her hair and makeup done.

"Oh hey, Billy."

"Barbara, you look, umm, umm, superlative," Billy stuttered.

Without a moment's notice, Kurt came from behind Barbara, grabbed her waist, and kissed her cheek. "Yeah, *my girl* got it going on." He held out his hand and introduced himself.

Billy reluctantly shook his hand as Barbara removed Kurt's arm from around her waist.

"It was nice to meet you, Bill."

"Umm, that's *Billy*."

"Billy, Bill, whatever." Kurt shrugged his shoulders nonchalantly and asked Barbara if she was "ret to go" tutor him. Barbara was embarrassed and wanted to correct Kurt, but not in front of Billy. She was not his girl, although she agreed to go out on a date with him *only* if he got his car out of the shop. But that was it, nothing more and nothing less.

"It was good seeing you," Barbara said as she and Kurt walked into study room number one.

Barbara closed the door for privacy, as well as to give Kurt a piece of her mind.

"What was that?"

"What was what?" Kurt asked, as if he was oblivious to the fact that he'd called her *his girl* and grabbed her waist.

"I'm not your girl."

"Yeah, not now, but you will be in the near future." Kurt's arrogance was at an all-time high as he pulled out his chair and sat down. Barbara rolled her eyes and thought *not in your wildest dreams*. But she kept it professional and asked Kurt to open his book so that she could get him out of her way for the day. He obliged.

Billy reflected on the interaction between Barbara and Kurt and thought to himself, *what was she doing with someone like him? She deserves better than that ghetto rabbit. An Ole, wannabe Bobby Brown scrub.* It was like Barbara and Kurt were from two different planets. Billy thought, *girls love losing with losers.* But of course, Billy Daye, he was a *winner*, and winning Sasha was his priority, not Barbara or that *Kurte*nstein.

"Hi Billy, I'm ready for you. You can come on back," Sasha said as she guided Billy across the room from Barbara and Kurt and led him to study room number seven. She walked ahead of him and her backside must have had his full attention because she stopped, and he continued, and bumped right into her. He apologized and she smiled while he took in her full beauty. She closed the door, and their tutoring session began.

Sasha knew the lesson plan because she and Billy took Mrs. Wilson's class together. She began writing problems on the whiteboard and explaining different ways of solving them. Billy sat there in silence, taking in her words and not paying much attention to the whiteboard. In fact, what Sasha taught he already knew because of Barbara. He didn't want to be rude or make Sasha feel like she wasn't doing a great job, but his session with Barbara was better. She taught him well and his only objective now was to get next to Sasha. He wanted more than tutoring. He wanted to get to know her, *all of her.* His mind ventured off many times during the session and he tried his best to be discreet. But he wanted Sasha and he was going to stop at nothing to get her, even if that meant pretending to be a "dumb jock."

"Billy, you are awfully quiet. Are you still following, or am I going too fast?"

"Oh no, keep that same pace."

"Do you have any questions?"

"Yes, what are you doing Friday night?"

"Are you asking me out?"

"Umm, yeah, that's exactly my intent."

"I don't know. I would have to think about it because I know you have a game on Saturday—"

"And?" Billy retorted, interrupting what she was about to say. He didn't want any reasons or excuses as to why she couldn't go out with him.

"I tell you what, I'm going to write an equation on the board. If you get it right, then it's a date." Sasha found what would be a difficult equation, one that they hadn't gone over. Billy walked to the board and kindly removed the dry erase marker from her hand. He looked at the equation and reflected on the tutoring session he had with Barbara, and how she made algebra *breviloquent*. She made it concise like when speaking, treated math in the same manner as speech. He continued staring at the board to solve the equation and began writing numbers that required only two lines, and the answer was on the second, last line. Sasha watched in amazement. She had thought for certain that Billy wouldn't be able to solve it. He finished working the equation, turned to Sasha, handed her the marker and winked. The wink caused Sasha to tremble inside, but she kept her cool. She saw Billy in a different light than she had prior to the tutoring session. He wasn't like the other *dumb* jocks. He was a lot smarter than he led her to believe. She was impressed.

She took the marker from Billy and placed it up against her cheek while her tongue made a bubble inside her inner left cheek. She couldn't believe he got the equation correct, and in a short time span. She turned toward Billy and said, "Well, I guess it's a date." Billy gleamed inside but he kept his cool and asked what time he should pick her up. She stated seven p.m. and asked where he was taking her, but he wouldn't say. "It's a surprise." She took out a piece of paper and wrote her number on it. He took the paper and asked, "You sure this is the right number?"

Sasha giggled and said, "Billy, you're crazy. Yes, it's the right number." She smiled and could hardly wait, and neither could Billy. He packed his book bag and asked if she needed a ride home. She declined, saying she had another session and her stepfather was coming soon after it ended. He bid her farewell and walked out of the room. He couldn't wait to collect his dinero from Wilt.

As Billy was leaving the study hall, he watched Kurt and Barbara's interaction with one another. He gasped, shaking his head in disappointment. Barbara was laughing at one of Kurt's theatrics.

"Funny guy, I see," Billy murmured to himself. He pushed open the double doors and headed toward his car. He heard someone calling his name and saw Wilt jogging to catch up with him.

"Hey man, so how did it go?"

Billy held out his hand and said to put his money right here, pointing to the inside of his palm.

"Nuh un, man, you're lying."

"I'm taking her out tomorrow night."

"Shut up. You're lying."

Billy pulled out Sasha's phone number and Wilt recognized her penmanship.

Wilt put his cuffed hand up to his mouth and began saying, "You're the man."

"The who? What did you say?" Billy asked as if he couldn't hear him.

"I said, YOU'RE THE MAN." Wilt said.

They laughed hysterically and didn't notice Barbara had come close enough to hear them.

"But I don't remember us shaking on the bet, so *I'm the man*."

"Man, whatever, I knew not to make a bet with you. You either broke or never pay up."

Billy slightly pushed Wilt on his shoulder and Wilt asked if he could get a ride home. Billy wanted to know what he was still doing at school and Wilt explained that he was in the gym lifting weights, but he'd wanted to know if Sasha was going to be a no-show.

"You asking me for a ride after you ain't paying your dues?"

"Come on, Billy. It ain't like that."

"It is like that. You better be glad I've known you my whole life, or else you would need a bus card and a transfer." Billy joked.

He and Wilt got in the car, and when they turned the corner on Main Street, he saw Barbara sitting on a bench at the bus stop. She didn't see him because her head was planted in a novel. He pulled right in front of her and honked his horn, startling her because she was temporarily in another world. She jumped, and her book landed on the ground. She looked up to see Billy and Wilt laughing. She didn't think it was *funny,* so she adjusted her eyeglasses and asked Billy what he wanted. He motioned for Wilt to get out and get in the back seat. Wilt was in disbelief because it was supposed to be bros before hoes, but Barbara wasn't a hoe, so Billy told him to get in the back seat or get out. Reluctantly, he scowled and got into the back seat. Billy motioned for Barbara to get in and she asked why?

"Girl, if you don't get in, it's going to be dark pretty soon and there's a lot of Dahmer's out here." She laughed, reflecting on yesterday's ride home and their conversation about cutting off heads and Jeffrey Dahmer. She looked at the sky and it was getting dark and cloudy, as though there would be more rain soon. She got up from the bench and got into the car. She closed the car door and Billy drove off. Kurt was running to the bus stop to catch up with her, but he saw her getting in Billy's car.

"Barbara, this Wilt, Wilt, this is Barbara."

They greeted each other cordially, even though Wilt was still upset about giving up his seat.

The car ride was a little melancholic and no one had much to say after the introductions. Billy turned to make a left to drop Wilt off at home first even though Barbara's house was the closest. Wilt didn't know where Barbara lived, but no matter the distance, he expected her to be dropped off *first*. Wilt sensed that Billy must have a "thing" for Barbara, so he began flirting with her to see Billy's reaction. He nudged the back of her seat and asked, "So, Barbara, you got a man?"

Billy looked through his rearview mirror at Wilt and wondered about his motive for asking her that question. But before Barbara could respond, Billy pulled up to Wilt's house and said, "All right, get out." Wilt didn't know if Billy was upset about the bet or him flirting with Barbara.

"Put yo claws in, man."

Billy put the car in park and emphasized, "Peace, man."

Wilt smirked, opened the door, and got out of the car. He slammed the door and leaned into Barbara's window, holding his hand out. He said it was nice meeting her and he hoped to see her around school. Barbara gently shook Wilt's hand with a smile of endearment and responded with "likewise."

"Wilt, slam my door again."

"My bad, man. Damn." Wilt looked Barbara in her eyes and smiled. She smiled back but quickly lowered her head like a shy schoolgirl. Wilt tapped the car door and told her to "take care." He looked at Billy with a sinister smile and turned to laugh as Billy sped away. Wilt watched the car disappear around the corner and proceeded to walk inside his home.

Billy couldn't wait to get Wilt out of his car. He was beginning to rattle his patience. He apologized for Wilt's lack of manners and Barbara replied that there was no need to apologize. She thought Wilt was kind of cute and had noticed him around campus.

"So, you like to read?"

"I *love* to read," Barbara emphasized love.

"What were you reading when I pulled up on you?"

"Tar Baby."

"Tar Baby? Isn't that a derogatory term for dark-skinned people?"

"Yes, it is, but the author turns the negative into a positive and it's a nice love story."

Barbara looked in her book bag to pull out the *Tar Baby* novel but noticed it wasn't there. She had forgotten to pick it up from the ground when Billy scared her and she dropped it. She was disappointed because the novel was just getting good.

"What's wrong? It seemed like you just saw a ghost in your book bag?"

"I left my book at the bus stop when you honked your horn."

"We can go back and get it."

Barbara insisted that it was okay; she had to get home and start dinner. Billy felt bad because he scared her and offered to buy dinner and go back for her book.

"Billy, you are so benevolent."

There she goes using those big words again. Why can't she talk like normal people and not like Webster's dictionary?

"I really don't mind, and I was the reason for you leaving it anyway."

"Well, in that case, we can stop and get veggie burgers at Earth Burger."

"I will take *you* to get veggie burgers."

Billy asked for the directions because he had never heard of Earth Burger. Barbara gave him the location and they were on their way to get veggie burgers. He remembered her stance and she had a good reason because of the slaughtering of the animals, but he wasn't ready to give up his steaks and potatoes. Those two foods went hand in hand. If he had to give up one, then he had to give up both, and that never was going to happen.

Twenty minutes later they pulled up to Earth Burger. Barbara received a text notification, took out her phone, and read that her father was working late and not to wait up for him. He would pick up something to eat after work, so she didn't need to cook. She was disappointed and sighed. She was always left alone because of her father trying to acquire this *big* promotion. She wished she had a sibling or her mother, because at times, she felt so alone.

"Do you want to eat here or get it to go?" Billy asked, trying to remove Barbara from her pity party, even though it was her reality. One that she'd loathed ever since she was ten years old.

"My father won't be home until later, so we can eat here if you don't have any plans."

"Naw, I don't, but I don't know about this food," Billy said as they pulled into Earth Burger. He shook his head from side to side, meaning, "no way" this was not him.

Billy got out of the car and went to open the door for Barbara as they proceeded to walk into the fast-food restaurant. They walked up to the counter and she ordered a veggie burger, fries, and a Coke. Billy didn't want anything; just looking at the menu made him cringe. He paid for the order and the food was ready five minutes later as they sat at the back of the restaurant to get a panoramic view of the outdoors. Soft old-school R&B music played over the sound system as The Spinners harmonized "Could It Be I'm Falling In Love" and Billy began to think about Sasha. He looked directly at Barbara and she smiled. He smiled back. "You sure you don't want to try this delicious burger?" Barbara held her burger within inches of Billy's mouth trying to persuade him to at least try it. He kept pushing her hand away saying he doesn't want any of that nasty meatless burger. Her persistence won him over. He took a small bite, chewed and swallowed, and grabbed his throat like he was going to throw up.

"You're so silly, it's not that bad."

"Speak for yourself," he said as he continued to gag. He grabbed her Coke without asking but she didn't mind. He opened the lid and drank until the taste of the burger was gone. He then let out a loud belch. Barbara laughed hysterically and called him "gross."

After catching his breath, he watched Barbara's mouth devour the burger, but not aggressively. More in a hungry and sensual way. Then she put ketchup on her fries, eating slowly one by one. He could watch her eat all night. The way she ate was unique and he wasn't sure if she was frontin' for etiquette reasons, but nonetheless, he thought it was cute.

"So, how did the tutoring session go with my cousin?"

"Huh?" She caught him off guard with the question about Sasha. His mind was on the art of *her* eating.

"You know, tutoring with Sasha?" she reiterated.

"Oh yeah, it was cool." He cleared his throat.

Barbara put a fry into her mouth, and he continued to watch like he was in a trance.

"What?" she asked. "Why are you looking at me like that?" She giggled due to shyness.

"Like what?" he asked, still in his reverie.

"Looking at me like a veggie burger." She teased.

This took him quickly from his daydream. "Oh naw, I was just looking at you. I don't know how to say it."

"Just say it."

"Are you sure you want to know? I mean, I don't want to embarrass you."

"Billy, just say it." She rolled her eyes and gently patted his hand.

"Umm, you got some ketchup on the side of your mouth."

She laughed with embarrassment and grabbed one of the napkins to wipe her mouth. Billy took the napkin from her hand and wiped another area of her mouth, totally opposite of where the ketchup had been. He said, "Now, that's better," and winked.

His eye wink was deadly, but in a good way. It was damn right sexy. She winked back, except with her wink, she looked like a smiling Cheshire cat. They continued to laugh and talked about family. Billy talked about his mother and sister and the loss of his father and Barbara talked about her father and the abandonment of her mother. And then their conversation turned to Sasha and Kurt.

"You never said how the tutoring session went with my cousin."

"I did. I said it was cool."

"Yeah, but that's not telling me much."

"Well, what do you want to know? And besides, what's up with you and Bobby Brown's little brother, Kurt?"

"Oh no, you didn't." She laughed.

"Oh yes, I did. You can do better than him."

She explained her relationship with Kurt in two seconds but skillfully put the focus back on her cousin.

"I mean, it's no secret you have the *hots* for my cousin. Did you get her number and ask her out?" Billy didn't know how to answer that because he was having such a good time with her that Sasha wasn't his focus *right now*. "Girl, why are you trying to be all up in my business like that?"

"Trust me, I'm not. I'm just asking like a concerned friend."

"Oh so, we're *friends* now?" He cracked a crooked smile and anxiously awaited her response. She began to eat another fry and washed it down with the small amount of Coke that was left from Billy's gagging incident. She held the cup to her mouth, trying to grab an ice cube with her teeth, and mumbled something inside the cup. He couldn't understand her, so Billy took the cup from her mouth and asked her to repeat it.

"I mean, I *guess*, we are friends." She hunched her shoulders and began to blush. They looked into each other's eyes and she quickly turned away and focused on her next fry. He teased her about how long she was taking to eat a small size fry. She threw one at him as he grabbed three of her fries, placed them in his mouth, and began to talk like he had cigarettes hanging from his lips.

"Stop it, you're wasting my fries." She grabbed her stomach from laughing so hard. Billy laughed as well and they both lost track of time. Barbara looked down at her watch and remembered that she had an English exam the next morning and needed to get home to study. Billy understood. He cleaned the table with a napkin and emptied her tray in the trash bin before they left, heading to her house. They pulled up to her home twenty-five minutes later and the lights were off again. This time, instead of waiting for Barbara to go inside and turn them on, signaling him to leave, he got out of the car, opened her door, and walked her to the front door. She unlocked it and turned on the lights, thanking him for dinner. He looked into her eyes and said, "No need to thank me, that's what *friends* are for." She thought to herself, *friends. And if he winks, too, I'm literally going to die*. She braced herself and there it was, Billy Daye's wink as he bid her goodnight. She closed the door and leaned her back against it, slowly sliding to the cold hardwood floor.

Chapter Five

Barbara sat at the breakfast table eating her bagel and getting her last-minute studying in for the exam. Her father unlocked the front door and walked inside looking disheveled. He had not come home for the night. He was hoping to make it home before Barbara left for school. He quietly closed the door and began rapidly walking to his room to shower.

"Where have you been?" Barbara came from around the corner and met him before he made it to his room. She asked with her hand on her hip, watching her dad fidget like he had been caught sneaking into the bedroom window. "Oh, hey Pumpkin." He turned and smiled with a look like he'd been caught with his hand in the cookie jar. She repeated her question and he dumbfoundedly hadn't come up with an explanation, but why should he? He was the adult and Barbara would be too in a few more weeks.

"You know, I'm trying to get this promotion and time escaped me. I fell asleep at the office. Sorry sweetie, you know I love you and I'm trying to do what's best for the both of us."

"Hmmm-hmmm. If so, then love should have brought you home last night." The minute she said that, laughter filled the room. One of Barbara's favorite movies was *Boomerang*. Leon was relieved by her satire because it gave him the escape he needed. In fact, she provided it because of the look of embarrassment on her father's face. He was a great father, a hard worker, and a provider. He deserved to have a late night with whomever the mystery lady was because she didn't believe her dad fell asleep at work.

"I got forty-five minutes to get showered and head to work, may I be excused?"

Barbara kissed her father on the cheek and whispered, "Have a good day."

She left to let her father get ready for work and catch her bus. While at the bus stop, she noticed Kurt wasn't there, but minutes later he drove up to the bus stop honking at Barbara and telling her to get in. She couldn't believe it; he did have a car. Kurt put the car in park and hopped out to open the door for her. She was reluctant to get in but did so anyway. Kurt jogged back to the driver side and they sped off, heading to school.

"Didn't I tell you I had a car?" Now, what you got to say?"

"I'm impressed, and I apologize for doubtin' you."

"Naw, all I want to know is where you want to go on our date tonight?" Kurt was on cloud nine. He got his car and his "girl," and explained to her how she never had to catch the bus again. Barbara was flattered but she didn't want to take him up on his offer because she wasn't "his" girl. He knew she wasn't, but he wanted to keep her far away from Billy Daye. He saw her get into his car yesterday and picked up the book that she left at the bus stop. He knew he had to get his car, and when he called the shop to inquire about the status, to his surprise, it was ready. He had his mother drive him to pick it up. He couldn't wait until today to pick Barbara up and drive her to school.

"How about you surprise me?"

"So, you're saying you are down for whatever?"

"I didn't say that, but I want to see your creativity." Kurt began stroking his goatee, barely any hair on his face and thought about where he was taking her. He pushed play on his radio and the sounds of Kenny G serenaded them through the speakers. Barbara watched and listened with amazement. She thought Kurt was putting up this hardcore persona but deep down, he was sensitive and compassionate, not a wannabe Bobby Brown. She looked at his features. His Cocoa complexion looked as smooth as a baby's bottom. She wondered if he had a skincare routine, or good genetics? She asked about his manicured hands and he laughed, telling her that his mother was an herbalist and created different types of herbs specifically for melanated skin. He was also a vegan and watched his diet.

"You're a vegan?"

"Yeah, I am. My entire family are vegans."

Barbara couldn't believe her ears. Kurt was full of surprises and she became more interested in finding out about him. She was looking forward to their date. She told him about being a vegetarian and they shared their favorite dishes. They arrived at school with smiles and laughter as he parked next to Billy's car. He hopped out to open Barbara's car door, grabbed her book bag, and retrieved his from the trunk. She was having such a good time with Kurt that she didn't notice Billy and Wilt standing a few feet away from the student parking lot.

"Hey, ain't that yo' girl?" Wilt asked Billy, pointing to Barbara and Kurt. Billy watched as Kurt threw both book bags across his shoulder and laughed along with Barbara. Billy smirked at Wilt, claiming that she wasn't his girl. Wilt knew his boy and knew that there was something special about Barbara. He had never thrown him out of his car behind a girl before. He didn't press the issue and felt bad for Billy, so he changed the subject to Sasha. Billy said that he and Sasha had a date that night.

"Stop lying."

"Why would I lie? I told you about the tutoring session when she gave me a math problem and made the bet about going out on a date. I won."

"Oh, is this a pity date or a you-won-a-bet date?"

"Does it matter? The point is, I will have Sasha all alone while you're hugged up with your blowup doll. What's her name, Zula?"

"Ahh, forget you. You always got weak-ass jokes."

Billy and Wilt went on and on with the jokes as both laughed until it was almost time for their first period. They did their handshake and parted ways. As Billy walked to his locker, he saw Barbara at hers and Kurt running his mouth. He couldn't comprehend why Kurt annoyed him, nor why it bothered him that

Barbara seemed to be enjoying his presence. He didn't know whether to interrupt or go to class. He slammed his locker and decided to walk to class, but changed his mind and made a U-turn on the way. Unfortunately, it was too late, Barbara and Kurt were no longer in sight.

Leon drove over the speed limit trying to get to work on time. He stopped at Starbucks to get an extra strong coffee. He didn't know if he could face Amber after last night, so he wanted to avoid her and the breakroom at all costs. He pulled into the parking lot and there stood Amber wearing a long overcoat with three-inch heels. Leon killed his engine and she walked to his car door. She wouldn't hardly let him get out of the car when she revealed what was underneath the coat. Leon couldn't believe it. He dropped his coffee, grabbed her hand, and took her around the corner of the building.

"Amber, what are you doing?"

"What does it look like I'm doing?" she asked as she unbuckled his belt.

"Amber, *no.*"

"No, what, huh?"

A noise coming from the south entrance of the building startled them both as they turned and saw a pair of headlights coming toward them. Their eyes grew big like a deer in headlights and instantly everything went dark when the lights turned off. Leon reached for Amber to check to see if she was okay and she was. He looked to the sky and silently thanked his God. They immediately picked themselves up off the ground and caught the elevator to the fourth floor.

"What the hell? Someone tried to kill us." Amber said, still half shaken by what had just occurred.

"I know, can you please calm down and where are your clothes?"

"In my frickin' bag." She patted her duffle bag to show where her clothes were located. The elevator dinged and Amber exited to the nearest ladies' room to change into her work attire. Leon watched her before going into his office. He placed his briefcase on the floor and walked to the breakroom to start the coffee machine.

Ten minutes later, he saw Amber exit the ladies' room, walk straight into her office without giving him a glance, and close her door. Leon sighed and continued walking to the breakroom. He turned on the light and started the coffee machine. He walked back to his office until it was ready and noticed that he had two missed calls on his cell phone. Both were from an unknown number. He placed the phone back on his desk and noticed Amber staring at him through the doorway. He sighed. His phone rang while she walked to the breakroom to pour a cup of coffee. On her way back to her office, she saw Leon on the phone talking to someone. He stopped talking when he saw her and closed his door for privacy. Amber gave a huff of disappointment and continued to her office with coffee in hand. She was bringing Leon a cup until he shut her out.

Leon ended his phone conversation and rubbed his head. He picked up his pen, pulled out a piece of notebook paper, and began to write a letter to his daughter.

Mrs. Wilson walked into the classroom and the class immediately got quiet. She had the results of yesterday's quiz in her hand. The results that would decide whether Billy played in tomorrow night's game. Billy looked at Sasha and she gave him a nod for reassurance that after what she taught him, he would be fine. He gave her a wink and his confidence was on an all-time high.

Sasha received her quiz, and as expected, she acquired a perfect score. Mrs. Wilson continued passing out the test. She stopped at Billy's desk and folded his paper for discretion. Billy hadn't seen her do this to the other student's papers, so his blood pressure rose about ten points from anxiety. He unfolded his paper and slid back into his chair, then sat upright and placed his test in his book bag. Mrs. Wilson continued with the lesson, and finally, the bell rang. Billy couldn't wait to talk to Barbara. He rushed out of the classroom with Wilt fast on his heels. He saw Barbara at her locker and was about to approach her, but Kurt got there first and grabbed her around her waist. From the looks of it, Barbara didn't seem to mind. She smiled and turned to see Billy standing behind her, with Wilt following.

"Hey, Billy," she said, noticing a piece of paper in his hand. She knew that his test results would be back today. He took his paper and began to put it back in his book bag.

"What up, Bill?" Kurt asked as he held his hand out to give him some dap. Billy looked at his hand as if it was invisible and then proceeded to walk away without a word. Barbara began walking after him calling his name several times before he turned to her.

"So, how did you do on the test?"

He took the test from his bag and gave it to her while walking toward the gym. She stopped to read the results and placed the test in her book bag, then began walking in the opposite direction. She met up with Kurt as they talked about their plans for that evening.

Wilt caught up with Billy in the gym and asked about his test results and Barbara. Billy didn't want to talk about either. He put on his football equipment and was ready to practice and take his frustration out on anyone on the field. Practice ended and after taking his shower Billy headed toward his car. His cell phone rang and it was Sasha. He smiled and picked up on the first ring. She was confirming their date for that night.

"Billy, wait up, man." Wilt called out.

Wilt jumped into the passenger side of the car before Billy took off.

"Wilt, man, not today. I have to get ready for Sasha tonight."

"Yeah, I know, but what up with you and Barbara?"

"Nothing is up with us, she tutored me and that's it," he said as he pulled out of the parking lot. Wilt didn't want to harp on it, but he saw more than a tutor. He hadn't seen Billy act this way since his last girlfriend, Lisa. He decided to change the subject to something more positive and brought up Sasha. He didn't even ask about the test results, figuring he was good to go since he practiced. Billy talked about where he was taking Sasha and Wilt asked if he could tag along. Billy asked, with who, meaning who would he bring with him? "Your blowup doll, Zula?" They both laughed.

"Man, screw you."

"Naw, but seriously, I want this to be all about Sasha and me. I want to get to know this girl *better*.

"All right, bet. I guess I will see you at the game tomorrow," Wilt said as he exited the car. He told him to call later and tell him about the date. Billy shrugged him off because he wouldn't kiss and tell.

Chapter Six

Kurt knocked on Barbara's front door and rang the doorbell. The door was slightly ajar and there stood Leon with his outstretched hand asking if he was Billy Daye. Kurt was taken aback because he wasn't Billy but how did he even know about him? His mind pondered for half a second and then he shook Leon's hand and introduced himself.

"No sir, I'm Kurt and I'm here to take Barbara out."

"Oh okay, well come on in." Leon was confused because Barbara never mentioned anything about *Kurt*. Leon asked Kurt to have a seat and the small talk began before Barbara came downstairs. Ten minutes later she entered, and Kurt couldn't thank God enough for her beauty *and* rescuing him from the job interview.

"What are your plans for tonight?"

Kurt couldn't tell him because it was a surprise for Barbara, so he said he was taking her somewhere to eat and hanging out with friends. Barbara avoided commenting because she knew it was a surprise date. She promised her dad that she would call him every hour if need be, and he assured her that it wasn't necessary and to have a great time. Before they left, he asked Kurt for a copy of his driver's license and Barbara exclaimed, "Dad."

"What?"

"Behave and don't wait up for me."

"Cinderella had a curfew and so do you, young lady. Be home by midnight, or else Kurt will turn into a pumpkin. Kurt laughed before wishing him a good night. Leon watched as Kurt opened the car door for his daughter and then drove away. He heard his cell phone ringing in the distance and gasped while locking the door and heading toward the kitchen to answer it. He looked at the caller ID, recognized the number, and answered. Her voice purred like a kitten and he was smitten as he took a seat on his sofa, propping his feet onto the ottoman. He lowered the volume on the Sports Center television broadcast and sang sweet nothings into the phone.

Twenty minutes later, Kurt and Barbara arrived at The San Antonio Museum of Art, and Barbara was indeed surprised. She had heard so much about it and wanted to attend. The museum was having an art party and many different artists and independent unknown artists were invited. Music and food were also included.

Barbara and Kurt admired many different artworks, especially the Black art, and after the display, they decided to get something to eat, and ended the night with dancing. It was ten o'clock and neither were ready to go home. Kurt pointed out that they had two more hours before he turned into a pumpkin and asked if she wanted to go to the skating rink. Barbara agreed and they headed to Goliad Street.

The skating rink was crowded as usual. They walked in and Roger and Zapp's song "More Bounce To The Ounce" boomed through the speakers. Barbara and Kurt rented their skates and began putting them on when she noticed her cousin and Billy hugged up in the corner of the rink. They were deep in conversation and hadn't noticed them when they walked in. After a few times around the rink, once in a couple's skate, Billy saw Kurt and Barbara hand and hand. Sasha followed his grin and noticed her cousin with a guy. She didn't personally know Kurt but had seen him around the campus at school. She tried to garner Billy's attention away from them by kissing him and he obliged. The couple skate ended, and as they exited the rink, Barbara went to the ladies' room and Kurt went to buy drinks.

Sasha entered the ladies' room soon after and as Barbara was washing her hands and checking her lip gloss, Sasha walked in to greet her.

"Hey cousin, what are you doing here?" Sasha asked.

"Oh, just hanging out with a friend."

"Friend? He seems like more than a friend since I've seen you with him on multiple occasions at school."

"Yup, he's just a friend," Barbara reiterated, and asked that she come join them at the table to introduce Kurt. Sasha took her up on her offer. She went to get Billy and they met at a table Kurt had reserved.

"Bill, what up?" Kurt exclaimed when he saw Billy. Billy shook his hand this time and corrected him with "Billy." Barbara introduced her cousin to Kurt. Kurt complimented Sasha on her beauty and how it ran in the family.

"It sure does." Billy placed his arm around Sasha as if to imply, "watch it, she's taken." But it was cool with Kurt because he was only interested in *Barbara*. He pulled Barbara close and pecked her on the cheek. It was an unexpected but nice gesture. Billy took it further and kissed Sasha on her lips. Sasha smiled, licked her lips, and asked, "So, how long have you all been dating?"

"We are..." Barbara began before Kurt pulled her up to skate with him to Freddie Jackson's "You Are My lady."

"I love this song," Kurt admitted while looking into Barbara's big brown eyes. He held her hand tight and sang along with the lyrics, "that said how their love will shine and make it last a lifetime." Barbara couldn't believe what she was feeling. Kurt had beyond surprised her and she was having a great time. The song ended and they joined Sasha and Billy back at the table. Except this time, Barbara sat next to Billy and he couldn't help but smell her sweet intoxicating perfume. He looked at her and she returned his glance with a smile.

He mouthed "thank you."

She asked, "For what?"

"Helping me pass algebra."

"It was all you. No need to thank me."

Sasha cleared her throat and asked where her appreciation was, since she tutored him as well. Billy laughed, stroked her face, and said that he already knew the problems prior to her session. He just wanted to get next to her.

"Did it work?" she asked.

"You're here with me, aren't you?" Billy then turned his attention back to Barbara as if Kurt or Sasha didn't exist.

"So, what did you do with my quiz?"

"I framed it." Billy cracked up laughing as Kurt interrupted their small talk and asked her if she was ready to go because he didn't want to turn into a pumpkin. It was time for him to return Cinderella before Leon put out an APB (all-points bulletin) on his ass. Barbara laughed and took Kurt's hand as they bid Billy and Sasha farewell for the night. They were returning their skates when Billy came to Barbara and asked if he could speak with her for a minute. He pulled her to the side and close because of the music and whispered in her ear, "How about another tutoring session to make sure I got it?"

"Sure, why not?" She beamed. Billy smiled and assured her with his infamous wink. Sasha and Kurt saw their exchange and didn't like it, but there was nothing either of them could do.

Minutes after Barbara and Kurt left so did Billy and Sasha. He walked Sasha to her front door and kissed her good-night. She asked when they were going out again, and he said, soon.

Kurt opened Barbara's car door and they talked for a few minutes about the art show and how much fun they both had and agreed to go on another date next Friday. When Kurt was about to kiss Barbara on the mouth, Leon opened the door and said, "it's eleven fifty-nine, Cinderella."

"Dad." Barbara exclaimed with a smile.

"Goodnight, Kurt," Leon said.

"Goodnight, sir, and thank you for entrusting me with your beautiful daughter."

"Goodnight, Kurt, and I will see you at school on Monday."

Leon closed the door and Kurt got into his car and sped away, but he couldn't help but notice Billy's car parked on the other side of the street at the neighbor's house. He slid down as Kurt passed by. Kurt made a U-turn to see if it was Billy but by the time he turned around, the car had vanished into the night. He didn't know if it was his imagination or not.

Billy pulled into his driveway and opened the front door. His mother was lying on the sofa with a photo album on top of her stomach. There were pictures of his father and their wedding day everywhere. A few had dropped on the honeysuckle wool carpet. He reached down to pick them up and placed them into the photo album. He put the album on the cedar coffee table and didn't know whether to wake his mother, so he removed her house slippers and covered her with a blanket. He kissed her forehead and whispered, "I love you, Mama. You gon' be all right."

He went upstairs and checked on his sister. She was sound asleep. He entered his room and turned on the light, but instead of going to sleep, he popped in the video to watch his last week's game. He watched his position and foot movement as he threw the football. It looked like he was throwing a piano and overthrowing his receivers. Wilt was open in the flat but he didn't see him. Billy kept rewinding the video over and over like he was in a trance while staring into outer space. After two hours and one hundred rewinds, he was sound asleep. The television static woke Brandy, who came into his room and shut the TV off. She didn't wake him because she knew he had a big game tomorrow and she needed her brother to perform like no other, since she and her friend were going to be there. Her reputation was on the line just as much as his. She turned off his light and closed the door.

Brandy's phone notified her that she had a missed call, and a text:

"Are you awake?"
"Olivia, what do you want at this time of the morning?"
"Can I call you?"
"No, I'm about to go back to bed. I will see you at the game tonight."
"All right then, bye."

Brandy was too sleepy to deal with Olivia's foolishness. She knew that a phone call would turn into an all-nighter. She wasn't trying to be rude, but she knew her girl. She remembered the time Olivia had a crush on her brother and she didn't want to relive that nightmare.

Before she fell asleep, she pondered what Olivia wanted, but thought that it could wait until tonight. She glanced at her alarm clock and it appeared like she didn't get any sleep. When she opened her eyes again, the clock read ten a.m. She pulled back her covers and rushed into the shower. She had an appointment to get her hair flat ironed. After her shower she got dressed and was going downstairs when she ran into her brother.

"Where are you going in such a hurry?" Billy asked.

"I'm going to see if mom could give me a ride to the salon."

"Mom is sleeping in today. I can give you a ride if you give me a minute." Brandy really wanted it to be her mom because she wanted to talk to her about something, but if Billy was willing to take over duties for the day, who was she to turn him down? Especially when her appointment was within thirty minutes.

Ten minutes later Brandy and Billy were on their way to the salon. She asked about Billy's status for that night's game and he assured her that he was clear to play and he would be starting. She warned him that he better "kill it" because she and Olivia would be there watching. Billy let out a gasp at the mention of Olivia's name. He remembered how she came on to him by disrobing herself while lying in his bed one night after he came home from practice. He'd covered his eyes and told her to put on her clothes. He was dating Lisa at that time, and he wasn't interested in his little sister's best friend.

"My reputation is on the line, so you need to do good."

"Girl, what are you talkin' about? You ain't got no rep." Billy laughed.
She was barely a sophomore and hadn't had enough time in high school to have one, but according to her, she did have one. Her star quarterback brother needed to keep it intact. Billy teased his sister until he pulled up to the salon and she got out and slammed his car door. She loved her brother, but he knew how to grind her gears and today was one of those days.

When Brandy entered the salon, it was crowded with hardly any room to sit. Crying babies and kids waiting for their mothers didn't make the packed shop any better. Barbara sat in a chair getting her hair done and noticed Brandy when she walked in. She had seen her getting out of Billy's car at school, but she didn't know their relationship.

Brandy located a seat near the water fountain close to the restrooms. She watched Barbara looking at her from head to toe. Brandy pretended not to see her and kept her attention on her phone, but every time she looked up, Barbara kept watching her.

"Excuse me, but do you know me?" Brandy asked.

Barbara immediately began staring at the wall above Brandy's head and Brandy turned around to see if there was anything that could have Barbara's full attention. Barbara cleared her throat and said, "I'm sorry. I didn't mean to stare, it's just that I have seen you before at school getting out of Billy Daye's car."

"Yeah, you have. That's because he's my brother."

"Oh, I see the resemblance. I'm his math tutor, Barbara Knight."

Brandy chuckled and said, "Oh wow, it's nice to meet you." Brandy walked up to Barbara and shook her hand, then quickly sat back down before she lost her seat. Brandy and Barbara began talking like they had known each other for years. She invited Barbara to the game, and she accepted. They exchanged numbers and home addresses so that she and Olivia could pick her up.

Barbara was done and Brandy had been called to the shampoo area before they bid their farewells. Two hours later Brandy's hair was fried, dyed, and laid to the side. Her mother arrived shortly, took one look at Brandy's hair as she entered the car, and said, "Brandy, what in the world?"

"Mama, don't even start with me. I know what you are going to say and that's what I wanted to talk to you about this morning, but Billy gave me a ride to the salon because you were sleeping in." Melody touched her hair and then looked at her hand. She wanted to know how soon the auburn dye could be washed out of Brandy's hair.

"Is it permanent?" Her mother asked.

"Mama, no, it's temporary."

"Oh, thank God."

Brandy said it was temporary but she wanted to get her approval to make it permanent.

"I mean, it's not awful. It's just that, it's too loud. Maybe tone it down a bit and it will be fine." Brandy pulled out a sample of the permanent color that she wanted, which Melody liked better and approved of. She hugged her mother and thanked her.

They went out to eat at Saltgrass Steak House before heading home. Brandy wanted to ask her mother if she was going to the game that night but knew she thought football was too violent and didn't want to see her son get hit. It was a fear that she carried ever since he became interested in football. She and Billy Sr. would disagree about the violent sport and she often worried her son would be carried off the field. She couldn't interfere with his dreams, but she didn't want to be there if it ever happened. She would sit at home, light a candle, and pray for his health. When the game was over, she would look to the sky and thank God for her son's safe return home. Little did she know that he was playing football so he could take care of her, so she would never have to work again. It was why he stayed up at night watching films and daydreaming. He wanted to take care of his family; a promise he had made to his deceased father.

Chapter Seven

Brandy, Barbara, and Olivia arrived at the game late and sat close to the cheerleaders.

"T.A.K.E take that ball away. Hey, hey, hey," the Buffalo cheerleaders sang as the opposing team was marching toward the goal line to tie the score. It was almost halftime and the score was Buffaloes seven and the Hurricanes zero.

Billy sat next to the quarterback's coach looking at a piece of paper. They could see Billy shaking his head and pointing at the paper. He and the coach were deep in thought and didn't see Brandy arrive. She yelled to get her brother's attention, but he couldn't hear her. She yelled again. Wilt heard her and walked over to Billy to show him that Brandy was calling him. Billy turned his attention toward the bleachers and saw Sasha leading the cheerleaders with a huge smile. He noticed Olivia, and then saw Barbara when she reached over to give her cousin a hug. He wondered what Barbara was doing there, and most importantly, what she was doing with his sister? Barbara sat back down and noticed Billy was looking in her direction. She gave him a thumbs up. He returned the gesture with a smile and Sasha did too. Except, Billy's gesture was for Barbara.

The crowd cheered as the ball was intercepted and returned to the twenty-yard line with thirty-five seconds until the half ended. The Buffaloes had one timeout remaining. Billy picked up his helmet and jogged to the field. He huddled with his team and called the play. "Cowboys deluxe" on three. All eleven offensive players clapped their hands and lined up at their respective positions. The ball was hiked to Billy. He rolled right and saw Matt wide open, but he couldn't stand him. He then saw Wilt open on the left side in the flat, with the clock winding down. He threw the ball to Matt and he dropped it. The crowd was shouting and gasped when the ball hit the ground.

When Billy got back to the huddle, he called Matt out, and they began arguing. Wilt pulled Billy aside to let him know they didn't have time for this. Billy agreed and then called the same play. Matt disagreed with the call but Billy didn't care, there was no way he was trusting him again.

The ball was hiked and instead of running to the right, Billy ran to the left and Wilt ran to the right side of the field. There was a defender in Billy's face, chasing him, and as soon as he threw the ball to Wilt, the defender hit Billy hard. He fell to the ground. Wilt caught the ball and began running toward the goal line for the score. He hurdled over the defender at the five-yard line and leaped into the endzone. The crowd went into a roar as Billy lay flat on his back. He heard the crowd roar, and threw up his arms. Billy's offensive lineman helped him to his feet and asked if he was okay as Billy nodded in pain. He held his right rib cage and gently jogged into the locker room, but he didn't leave without looking up at the stands. He saw Barbara standing with her hands over her mouth, concerned about his health. She gave him a thumbs up and he returned his signature gesture as he removed his helmet and gave her a wink. By the time the game ended Billy was the hero. He had thrown for another two-hundred yards and three touchdowns after halftime, and the Buffaloes never looked back.

Billy took the game ball and wrote "get well soon" and "8-0," dedicating it to Coach Walker.

The team erupted in cheers and chanted "eight and zero."

Thirty minutes later, after a cold shower, Billy and Wilt got dressed, and into Billy's car and decided to go get a bite to eat to celebrate the victory. Billy phoned his mother to let her know that he would be home late and would be eating out. He asked if his sister made it home, but she hadn't. He pondered where she could be, wondering if Barbara was with her.

"Okay. Mom, I love you," he said as he hung up the phone.

Immediately after talking to his mother, his cell phone rang, and it was Sasha. He answered on the third ring after turning down the music.

"Hey, you." Billy said.

"Hey, what are you up to?"

"Nothing, I'm just chillin' with my boy, Wilt." Wilt tried to grab the phone because he wanted to know who Billy was talking to. Billy covered the receiver so Sasha couldn't hear the interaction, elbowing Wilt slightly in his upper chest.

"Oh, it's like that?" Wilt exclaimed with a hint of jealousy.

Billy kept talking to Sasha while ignoring Wilt as they turned into the restaurant parking lot. Billy agreed to meet up with Sasha as she purred into the phone, telling him that she would see him later.

"Man, who was that?" Wilt asked.

"Do I need to tell you *all* my business?"

"What happened to bros before hoes?"

"What? First, of all, Sasha ain't no hoe."

"Oh, so that's who was on the phone?" Wilt told Billy how these women got his nose wide open and that he better be careful. He didn't want another "Heartbreak Hotel" moment with him. Billy started laughing, remembering the time when Lisa broke his heart and he had gone to Wilt's house and played Michael Jackson's song. Followed by Gloria Gaynor's "I Will Survive." Wilt and his playlist for broken hearts had Billy feeling much better by the time he left. Every time he mentioned Lisa, Wilt would begin to sing one of his playlist songs to make him smile. Wilt was his best friend and couldn't stand to see him in such a pitiful state because of a girl. He knew how easy it was for him to fall in love, despite his *tough guy* exterior. Billy often referred to himself as a grizzly bear, but deep down inside, he was nothing more than a stuffed animal.

Billy and Wilt got out of the car and noticed a lot of their teammates were there hanging outside and playing music, talking about the game. They walked in and were greeted by fellow classmates, congratulating them. While Billy was ordering his usual burger, fries, and suicide (chocolate, vanilla, and strawberry) shake, he noticed a familiar voice. He turned to his right and saw Kurt bussing tables. He was talking to Barbara, who was sitting with Billy's sister and Olivia. Billy didn't know whether to frown or smile. He was happy to see Barbara but didn't like Kurt holding her attention and making her laugh. Barbara slightly touched Kurt's arm and held her stomach, laughing at his corny conversation. His sister was on her phone, and Olivia had her Mac lip gloss out and was holding a mirror, applying it to her lips. He watched them until the number for his food was called. He walked toward them to say, "What's up?" and get bozo the fool away from Barbara.

Wilt watched Billy in silence. It was like he wasn't even there with him. He said to himself, *my man is really buggin'*. Wilt grabbed his food and followed behind Billy to let him know that he had his back no matter what. After he'd greeted his sister, Barbara, and Olivia, Kurt yelled, "Hey Bill." as he reached to shake his hand. Billy ignored him, and he and Wilt continued walking to sit down at a table a few seats behind Barbara, his sister, and Olivia. After being dissed, Kurt picked his face up off the floor and continued talking to Barbara. Olivia looked at Wilt and smiled. He smiled back and raised his head in an upward position. She turned back around quickly.

"What's that all about?" Brandy asked as she nudged Olivia on the arm.

"Oh, you don't want to know because I tried to tell you about it last night, but you were *so sleepy*." Olivia rolled her eyes and sucked her teeth.

"Stop playing. I know you ain't crushin' on Wilt?"

Olivia looked down at her nails and began playing with them, ignoring Brandy.

"Girl, you're silly. I know you hear me. I'm going over there and asking him if you don't start talking." Brandy got up from her seat and began walking to sit with Wilt and her brother. Olivia tried to stop her, to no avail. She got to their table and asked her brother to scoot over so she could sit with him. He stood up, letting her in the seat and asked what she wanted. He asked about her hair and said he thought it looked kind of "fly" like a fly on the wall. Wilt chuckled and told her that she could wear a mop on top of her head and she would still look good.

"Thank you, Wilt," she said, and stuck her tongue out at her brother.

"Man, you need bifocals? Forget you."

After the jokes ended, Brandy pretended she was asking Wilt about Olivia, but actually she was congratulating them on a good game. She told her brother how he kept her reputation intact with his game play. Billy laughed because there she went again talking about her "sophomore reputation." She turned to Wilt and acknowledged his touchdown before halftime and how well it was orchestrated between him and her brother. She talked to them for another five minutes before returning to her table. When she got there, she noticed Kurt sitting next to Barbara, who laughed aloud like she was watching a Comic Relief show. She laughed so loud that it caught Billy's attention. He could hardly enjoy his meal, watching the exchange between Barbara and Kurt.

"What's up with that dude?" Wilt asked.

"What dude?"

"The one who called you Bill and you ignored him."

"Oh, that bozo? Nuttin', but he needs to keep his day job because his jokes are whack."

"I don't know. It seems like Barbara is his number one fan." Wilt was trying to see how Billy felt about her, so he continued talking about how much she appeared to be enjoying Kurt's company. He complimented her new hair style and how she was looking good these days.

"Yeah, she looks aight."

"Man, stop lying. You know she lookin' good." Wilt laughed because he was getting under his skin.

"You must have forgotten who I was talking to right before we pulled up?"

"Oh, that's right, Sasha. Now, that honey, oowee." Billy agreed, and they gave each other some dap on how fine Sasha was and the fact that he was supposed to meet up with her later, too.

Billy watched Kurt get up from his seat and gave Wilt the excuse that he was going to the restroom. Actually, he wanted to talk to Barbara. While on his way to the "restroom," he stopped and asked Barbara if he could talk to her for a minute outside. He had something to give her. Brandy and Olivia were in their own one-on-one conversation about what Olivia wanted to tell her the previous night, so they didn't notice Billy or Barbara leaving.

Billy held the door open and let Barbara walk in front of him. He led her to his car and complimented her hair and how nice she looked. She was smitten by his comments, and her behind swished like a swinging door. Billy watched in admiration, knowing that she put on a little more umph as he walked and opened the trunk of his car. Inside was an autographed football with Barbara's name, signed by him. She took the football and read the message written with a black sharpie: *You're the real MVP*. She looked surprised and covered her mouth in disbelief.

"What's this?" she asked.

"It's a football. Duh."

"I know that silly, but what's it for?"

"It's a game ball for *you* for playing an important role in helping me pass algebra. I couldn't have done it without you." Barbara began shaking. She was elated and didn't know whether to hug *and* kiss him. She knew that Kurt was inside the restaurant watching, but she didn't care because he wasn't her man. She reached her arms around Billy to give him a genuine hug and accidentally dropped the ball. Billy reached down to pick it up and placed it in her hands, and that's when someone came from behind Billy and grabbed him by the waist. He recognized who it was by her smell. Her Elizabeth Arden 5th Avenue perfume intoxicated him, and he couldn't get enough of it.

"Hey cousin, what are y'all doing out here? Billy, I thought you were with Wilt?" Sasha began questioning. She was looking very sexy in her cheerleading attire. He explained that Wilt was inside and he'd come to the car to give Barbara something for helping him pass math. Sasha looked at the football in Barbara's arms and asked where hers was? Billy took her into his arms and whispered in her ear. She giggled and turned to give him a push on his bicep.

Barbara watched their exchange and excused herself, saying that she better get back inside. Billy thanked her again and Sasha said, "Yeah cousin, good job teaching *my* man." She and Billy kissed and talked about their plans, and then she grabbed his hand and asked if he was ready to go. He needed to take Wilt home and then they could go to Sasha's house for a nightcap.

Sasha and Billy entered the restaurant a few minutes after Barbara to get Wilt and take him home. He introduced Sasha to his sister and Olivia and wished Barbara a good night before he left with Wilt and Sasha. He opened Sasha's car door, Wilt hopped in the back seat, and they drove off.

Chapter Eight

Barbara was awakened by the phone ringing. It was Sunday morning and she wanted to sleep in and study later for exams she had coming up that week. She was exhausted from the previous night. After the game she, Brandy, and Olivia went to eat, then she wished them farewell and left with Kurt to go cruising. She didn't get home until close to midnight. Her father wasn't home when she arrived, but he had texted to let her know that he was working overtime. He had to make extra money because her eighteenth birthday was fast-approaching and he wanted to surprise her with something that she needed. She couldn't wait and had no idea what he planned. She wanted a party or some kind of get together because she didn't know many people since transferring to Fox Tech.

"Dad, can you get the phone?" Barbara yelled but he didn't hear her because he was in the shower. Barbara reached over to answer, and someone hung up. She placed the phone back on the hook and covered her head. The phone rang again, but this time, Leon and Barbara answered at the same time.

"Hello?" Leon answered.

"I want to see Barbara. You are not going to keep me away from her, Leon."

"Listen, we'll do it when the time is right. But it's not right now. I will contact you. Please don't call here again." Leon immediately hung up the phone and began getting dressed. To his surprise, Barbara was standing in his doorway asking about the phone conversation.

"Who was *that* on the phone?"

"Someone from my job needing to go over the upgrade documentation."

"Dad, don't lie. I heard them on the phone."

"Pumpkin, I wouldn't lie to you. It was nothing important. You look exhausted. Go back to bed and get your sleep. I'm going to the office for a few hours and then I will be home."

Barbara didn't argue or question him. She did what she was told and went back to her room and got into bed. Except she couldn't sleep because of the phone call. She looked at the caller ID and noticed that the number was listed as "unknown." She pondered if she should push *69 to retrieve the last call. She picked up the phone receiver and heard her dad making plans to go over to a woman's house. She knew he wasn't going to work and was secretly seeing someone.

"I can't wait to see you, baby," the unidentified woman sang into the phone.

"Well, let me go so that I won't keep you waiting."

Barbara hung up the phone and pretended to be asleep when her dad came to check on her and tell her that he was leaving. He quietly entered her room and sat on her bed. He looked into her angelic, innocent face, and kissed her forehead. She smiled and said, "Have a great time. You shouldn't keep her waiting." He was busted *again*. He made amends by offering to go out later and spend some father-daughter time together when he returned, and she accepted. He walked out of her room, got into his car, and was on his way to his lady friend's home.

After hearing the car leave, Barbara picked up the phone and dialed *69. A young man answered the phone.

"Thank you for calling the Hilton Hotel in sunny California, how can I assist you today?"

"Um, who's this?" Barbara asked in her groggy voice.

"This is Anthony, how can I assist you?"

"Yes, what place of business is this?"

"The Hilton Hotel located in Los Angeles."

"Oh, someone called here about twenty minutes ago and I wanted to know who it was."

"I wish I could help you, but we have hundreds of guests and I couldn't provide you with that information." Barbara thanked the attendant and hung up the phone feeling defeated. She didn't know what was up with her father but knew he had been lying to her and keeping secrets. How could she confront him? Maybe she would get some answers that night at dinner.

Twenty-five minutes later, Leon was at Amber's home. She was at the door waiting for him and wearing a see-through negligee. He didn't knock or ring the doorbell before she swung the door open and immediately began kissing and disrobing him. He closed the door with his foot, and in between make-out sessions, she asked what took him so long. His response was "Good things come to those who wait." With that, she tore off his shirt and he picked her up and took her to the bedroom.

Two hours later she was in the kitchen making him a sandwich. They ate lunch, put in a DVD, and watched Leon and Jane Kennedy's movie, *Body And Soul.*

Amber lay in his arms and he held her tight and kissed the top of her head. He lightly massaged her scalp until she fell fast asleep and so did he.

Leon awoke and noticed that it was almost five p.m. He checked his cell phone and there were no calls from his daughter, which he was thankful for. He didn't want to wake Amber but he had to go. He made a promise that he would spend time with Barbara and he wanted to keep it. He lightly moved Amber to lay her on the bed and got up to take a shower. He was dressed within twenty minutes. He kissed her and locked the front door.

When he pulled out of the driveway, he noticed the same car that tried to run him and Amber over was following him. He looked through his rearview mirror to keep an eye on it. He didn't want to go home, so he made several turns until he lost the car. Then he dialed Barbara to see where she wanted to eat. She chose Spaghetti Warehouse. He said that he would be home within five minutes and that he was ready to leave as soon as he arrived.

Leon pulled into the driveway and Barbara rushed outside like a teenager on her first date. She looked beautiful and he noticed how his little girl was becoming a woman. He saw what Kurt and Billy saw in her and that frightened him.

Leon got out and opened the car door for her and they drove to their destination. He complimented how nice she looked and how the new straight with curls hairstyle suited her. They got out of the car and entered the restaurant. She wanted to sit inside the train to eat but Spaghetti Warehouse was so crowded there weren't any seats there. Barbara didn't mind waiting for a booth to become available, so she and her dad played a few video games until their name was called. Ten minutes later a booth in the train was waiting for them. They sat down and the waitress gave them menus and took their drink order. Barbara wanted water and so did her dad. They ordered and fifteen minutes later their food was ready. Barbara looked up as they began eating and saw Sasha walk inside. Sasha saw her uncle and cousin and waved to them. Seconds later, Billy walked in right behind her. Sasha took Billy's hand because she wanted to introduce him to her uncle.

"Hey Uncle Leon." she said as she bent down to kiss him.

"Sasha, wow, I haven't seen you in a while. You need to come visit more. I almost didn't recognize you."

"Uncle, this is my boyfriend, Billy Daye."

Leon almost choked as he wiped his mouth. He had heard Billy the star quarterback's name a lot, but always from his daughter's mouth and thought he was *her* love interest. He gathered himself together and shook Billy's hand.

"Aww, so you're Mr. Daye."

"Yes, sir." Billy shyly answered and held a tight grip as he shook Leon's hand. Billy looked at Barbara and she pretended not to notice the shock on his face. She began fiddling with her salad when Sasha suggested that they all sit together. Barbara noticed her father eyeing Billy up and down, trying to understand why Sasha was there with him, and why she'd introduced him as *her* boyfriend.

Leon stood up and sat next to his daughter to let Sasha and Billy sit next to each other. The waitress asked if they would be joining this table and they agreed. She took their order, and their food was ready within ten minutes.

Sasha was the center of attention and talked non-stop. No one could get a word in, but that might've been a good thing because Leon didn't want to have to explain the phone call made earlier to his home. Then again, he couldn't help but notice how uncomfortable his daughter was. He gently held her hand to assure her that everything would be all right. She squeezed his hand to say thank you.

"So, Billy, how did you and my niece meet?" Sasha didn't give Billy a chance to answer. She told him that they were in algebra class together and Billy needed a tutor, so she had taken up the role.

"But I thought Barbara was your tutor?"

"Yes, she was," Billy said. "And what a great job she did. She helped me pass my class and I was eligible to play in the game last night because of her."

"Well, that's my Pumpkin, she has always been a smart little cookie." Leon reassured his daughter by squeezing her hand again.

"Uncle, I taught Barbara everything she knows. Right, Barb?" Sasha continued to make everything about her. She hugged and kissed on Billy the entire time at nauseam. Barbara began getting irritated but stayed reserved. She loved her cousin and had always taken the back seat to let her shine. Billy noticed how uncomfortable Barbara looked. His eyes stayed on her and he didn't hear much of what Sasha was saying. He wanted to comfort Barbara and let her know how amazing she was and that she was the better tutor, but he didn't want to go there. Leon watched the body language between his daughter, niece, and Billy and could see that Billy was caught in the middle. He saw how Billy looked at his daughter. It was different than the way he looked at Sasha.

Barbara excused herself to go to the restroom and Billy continued to watch her. Sasha decided to go with her, even though Barbara wanted to get away from her cousin's mouth. Billy got up to let Sasha out and while they were in the ladies' room Leon and Billy sat and had a *real* conversation. Leon wanted to know Billy's plans after high school and what his intentions were with his niece. Leon was impressed by Billy's responses. He passed the vetting stage with flying colors.

Sasha and Barbara returned, and it was time to pay the bill and leave. Leon paid and left a nice tip for the kind waitress. Billy insisted that he would pay but Leon wouldn't let him. He knew that high school kids didn't have much money and would take care of it. Little did he know, Billy's father's insurance plan and pension had left him money for school, and he had been able to access it when he turned eighteen a few months ago. It allowed him to focus on sports and graduating from college, not only high school. He'd made his father a promise that he would earn a degree.

Sasha and Barbara led the way out of the restaurant followed by Billy and Leon. They hugged and Sasha kissed her uncle goodnight and promised not to be a stranger. Billy whispered to Barbara that they were still good, and asked if she was going to tutor him the next day. She told him not to be silly, that she would see him at five thirty sharp and for him not to be late. Sasha grabbed Billy's arm and they headed to the car. He opened her door and Barbara and Leon watched them drive off. Leon placed his arm around his daughter and walked to their car. They left, and on the way home, there were so many unspoken words that needed to be said, but they drove in silence. Barbara seeing Billy with her cousin and the secret phone call was too much to bear. She wanted it all to go away but she didn't know why she was feeling that way about Billy. He wasn't her man; he was Sasha's man.

When they arrived home, Leon noticed the same black car that had followed him from Amber's house was parked across the street from his home. He quickly opened the car door for Barbara and turned on the interior and exterior lights to make sure she was safe inside. As soon as she was through the door, the car blinked the headlights twice and sped away. The car's windows were tinted dark, and Leon couldn't see inside because he was blinded by the high beams. He shielded his eyes and stood there until the car was out of sight, then closed the front door, set the alarm, and went to check on Barbara. She was in bed looking at her phone when a text message came through.

"Hey, you. You all right?"

She didn't recognize the number, so she texted back asking who it was.

"Jeffrey Dahmer. LOL"

"Whatever, silly. Lol."

"My sister gave me your number. I hope you don't mind."

Barbara turned on her back with an enormous smile as she responded to Billy's text message.

Leon watched his daughter and slowly turned away seeing that she was *just* fine.

Chapter Nine

Kurt pulled into Barbara's driveway waiting to give her a ride to school. She immediately rushed out and kissed her father good-bye. He had met Kurt before so there was no need for another introduction. Leon stood at the door and waved good-bye. After Kurt and Barbara left, he walked to the side of the house to retrieve the trash bin because it was garbage pick-up day. He greeted nosy Mrs. Hopkins, the next-door neighbor, before retiring into the house to get dressed for work.

Thirty minutes later he headed out to get a breakfast bagel. He phoned Amber and asked if she wanted any breakfast, but her answer was not food related. Leon laughed at her response but couldn't wait until she was in his arms again. They made plans after work and he ended the call with, "See you soon, dear."

Leon got to work and immediately began finishing the final touches of Barbara's surprise birthday gift. She would be turning eighteen in less than a week and he wanted to make sure that everything was signed, sealed, and delivered on time. He phoned the company and said that he would be in during lunch to sign the paperwork.

A gentle knock sounded at his door.

"Come in," he said while still holding the phone receiver.

Amber sashayed into his office, sat in his visitor's chair and grabbed his bagel, and began to eat a small piece. She crossed her legs and then opened them wide to show Leon that she wasn't wearing any underwear. He immediately ended the phone call to ask what she was doing and if she was trying to get him fired. He got up and locked the door because he knew how aggressive and cavalier she could be. Their relationship was supposed to be between them only. But Amber loved living on the edge, on the wild side. At times, Leon loved it too, but he knew that he had more to lose than she did if they were ever caught. He often questioned why or how he got involved with Amber. His two heads were in cahoots with each other, but the lower half got the better of him. Her sex appeal and flirty ways had finally won him over after an entire year.

"Whatcha thinkin' about, Big Daddy?" She pulled his tie to get closer to him.

"I'm thinking about what I'm going to do to you tonight. But you need to pull yourself together in the meantime."

"Oh, I wanna know what you got for me and why can't I have it now?" She purred into his face.

A knock sounded on the door and they both jumped. She immediately let go of Leon's tie and straightened her mini skirt. It was housekeeping wanting to get into Leon's office to clean. Amber let Rebecca in and blew Leon a kiss before she left. He watched her behind leave and looked down to see his woody growing. He took his suit coat and slung it over himself as he headed to the men's restroom.

He returned and Rebecca was still in his office cleaning. She saw him walk in and gave him a disappointed look. "You know better than to be fooling around with her. She ain't nothing but trouble."

"Rebecca, mind your business. It's not what it looks like."

"Mmhmm. It's exactly what it looks like and don't say I didn't warn you." She took her cart and rolled her eyes before walking out of the office. Leon sat down in his chair and rubbed his head. He knew that Rebecca was right. He needed to end this fling between him and Amber quickly before it got out of control. He thought about breaking it off over dinner that night. He'd take her out and tell her that he no longer wanted to have anything to do with her unless it involved work. But he also knew he was walking a fine line if she didn't take it well. What if she got him fired? If he continued to go down the same path, it was bound to get back to the main boss that he was screwing the man's granddaughter.

He'd be violating company policies and that would determine his termination. He was damned if he did and damned if he didn't.

He thought about updating his resume and applying for other software engineering positions. He needed a back-up plan because he knew what he had gotten himself into wouldn't end well. He spent the entire morning applying for different positions, even out of state. Barbara would soon be going to college, so if he needed to travel or move, after graduation would be the best time.

After applying for jobs, he grabbed his jacket and was on his way to get a bite to eat and sign the paperwork for his daughter's birthday gift. Amber saw him rushing off and tried to stop him, but he ignored her. He quickly texted her that he had an appointment and that he would make reservations for dinner tonight. He knew that would pacify her and free him to run his errands without one hundred questions. She texted back with several emojis and wrote: "See you soon and I can't wait to have you to myself." Leon read the text and closed his phone. He didn't care to respond because it was over. He had to end it tonight.

Billy saw Barbara at the school cafeteria eating lunch with Kurt. He wanted to confirm their tutoring appointment, but didn't want to interrupt or make her feel that he was being a pest. Instead of walking up to her, he sent her a text.

"Hi, this is the mass murderer. I wanted to make sure that we r still on for 4 today? I promise I won't kill you, I mean bite."

Kurt had been talking Barbara's ears off until she got a text notification. She pulled her phone from her pocket and read it, then cracked up laughing and began looking around the cafeteria for Billy. She knew that he took his lunch at the same time but she didn't see him. Kurt wanted to know what was so funny and who she was looking for. She said no one and continued their conversation. A few minutes later, Sasha walked up and sat down to eat her lunch. She asked about Barbara's plans and Barbara told her she had tutoring after school that day. Sasha insisted she let her cover the tutoring because she knew Barbara had major exams and had to get ready for her birthday bash on Saturday.

"Oh, I wasn't invited? You ain't told me nothing about your birthday?" Kurt placed his hand on his hip and waited for her response.

"I hadn't told anyone, yet. It's just going to be something small and intimate. Nothing too outlandish," Barbara said.

"What time should I be there?" Kurt asked. Barbara didn't know, but said she would let him know by the next day. She asked Sasha not to mention it to anyone because she was only inviting a few of her classmates. Sasha placed her index finger and thumb together and ran them across her lips to say that her secret was safe and zipped.

"Anyway, I will take your tutoring session today so that you can study."

"Are you sure?"

"Cuz', I got you."

Barbara hugged her cousin and thanked her.

Billy finished practice with a bang. He was feeling good about his game play and had talked with Coach Walker, who was feeling much better and was home resting. He gave him nothing but accolades about how he played on Saturday. He was proud of him for bringing up his algebra grade and thanked him for the game ball. Coach planned to return to work in a few weeks and Billy couldn't wait. He had designed some plays but wanted to run them by him first.

Billy walked into the study hall, signed in, and sat in a chair waiting for Barbara to take him back to one of the rooms. He looked at his phone and noticed that he was ten minutes late. Barbara was a stickler when it came to being on time.

"Hey, babe. Are you ready?"

"Hey, Sasha. Ready for what?"

"I will be tutoring you today because my cousin had a lot of studying and she has to get ready for her birthday party, too." When Sasha said "birthday party," she immediately covered her mouth. She couldn't hold water let alone keep a secret. "Pretend like you didn't hear that. Okay?" Sasha warned that it was supposed to be a surprise. Billy wasn't paying much attention to anything that was coming out of Sasha's mouth because he was supposed to be tutored by *Barbara*.

Barbara and Kurt walked into the study hall and she immediately apologized to Billy that she forgot to let him know Sasha was going to take her place that afternoon. She told him not to worry and reiterated, "You will be in good hands with your *girlfriend*. Remember, she taught me everything I know?" The only thing was, Billy didn't concur with that statement. Barbara was by far the better tutor.

Kurt put his arm around Barbara, asked if she was ready to go, and they left. Billy stood there and watched until they disappeared out of sight. He wanted to punch Kurt right on his knuckle head, but Sasha placed her arm inside his, leading the way as he reluctantly walked to study room number one.

Sasha and Billy did more smooching than teaching, but it was fine with him because he no longer needed to be tutored.

An hour later, they pulled up in front of Sasha's home and saw that her mother was back from her business trip. Sasha decided it was time for her mother and stepfather to meet Billy. Billy didn't see the *relationship* through the same lens she did, but how could he deny the most popular girl in school by telling her she wasn't his girlfriend? Sasha was every high school boy's wet dream, but she was his reality, standing right next to him about to introduce him to her family.

"Are you sure you're ready to meet my parents?" Sasha reiterated because Billy seemed as jumpy as a June bug in a hen house. He tried his best to get himself together by taking a few deep breaths before answering.

"I'm as ready as I'll ever be." He sighed. She unlocked the front door and called out to her mother that she was home because she didn't want to startle her. A faint voice could be heard coming from the kitchen where her mother stood wrapped in her stepfather's arms.

"I'm in the kitchen," Elizabeth called out. Sasha and Billy walked in to find her mother cooking dinner and her stepdad doing a taste test.

"Mom and Dad, I want you to meet Billy Daye, the guy I've been talking your ears off about."

"Oh yes, the quarterback," Elizabeth said as she reached out to embrace Billy in a warm hug. He noticed she wore the same perfume fragrance as Sasha. Sasha and her mom looked more like twins than mother and daughter. She was maybe an inch taller than Sasha but had the same sparkling brown eyes and dimples. "Hi, Billy. I'm Sasha's father." Jimmy never considered Sasha a stepdaughter since he had raised her from infancy. Elizabeth had been pregnant with Sasha when they met. He had a strong grip as he shook Billy's hand. He must have been a captain in the military by his stature and demeanor. He stood over six foot four, tall, brown skinned with salt and pepper hair. His goatee was the same color as his hair. He looked much older than his wife, but he couldn't tell her age.

Billy wiped his sweaty hand on his pants leg and then accepted Jimmy's firm handshake.

"Nice to meet you, Mr. and Mrs. West."

"Oh, you can call me Mama Lizzy," Elizabeth said as she gestured in a *don't be silly* way, welcoming him into her personal space. Jimmy said for Billy to call him "Jim" because that was how his close friends and family referred to him.

Billy relaxed after seeing the warm and sincere personalities of Sasha's parents. He thought for sure that Jimmy would drill him like an Air Force recruiter and Elizabeth would ask what his intentions were with her daughter. But it was the complete opposite, and he was invited to stay for dinner. Billy declined since it was a school night and he had to study. He wanted to watch more football film to get ready for the next game. The West family understood and didn't keep him much longer. They ended with nice pleasantries and wished him luck at the game on Saturday.

Sasha walked Billy out to his car and invited him to dinner on Sunday. The West family had a tradition of inviting family, friends, and church members over for Sunday dinner each week. Billy accepted and kissed her goodnight, saying he would see her the next day.

Sasha skipped into the house like a giddy little schoolgirl. He watched her hips sway from side to side, waiting until she entered the house safe and secure before he left.

He thought to himself, *hmmm I'm Sasha's man.* He confirmed what she had already known a week ago.

"Me, Billy Wesley Daye Jr. I'm Sasha West's man." he shouted to himself and anyone who could hear him, though no one was around. He didn't care, the only thing he cared about and knew for certain was...

"I'm Sasha West's man."

He pushed play on his stereo and "Could It Be I'm Falling In Love" serenaded him through the car speakers. He sang loud and out of tune as he rewrote the lyrics to The Spinners' number-one hit song.

"Could it be I'm falling in love with you, Sasha?"

Chapter Ten

Leon and Amber sat in the corner of the Silo restaurant in a cozy area. The decor was debonair, with chandeliers hanging among the rafters and Black artwork uniquely placed above every other table. Amber was used to the best and Leon was aware of her expensive taste. They ordered red wine with steak, lobsters, baked potatoes, asparagus, and a salad. Leon preferred his steak medium sautéed and so did Amber. He took another sip of his Taylor Fladgate 40 red wine, gearing up to break the news to her. He didn't know whether to let her finish eating or tell her that it was over now, while waiting for the food.

Amber removed her left cream-colored stiletto and slowly began stroking Leon's leg under the table. Her toes felt so good. He took another sip of wine and envisioned making love to her. He snapped out of his reverie when he noticed his boss walk into the restaurant with his wife. His knee-jerk reaction baffled Amber as he pointed to the hostess welcoming Amber's grandparents. She sucked her teeth and said she didn't care, that she was a grown woman, and they were bound to find out about their affair.

"Amber, listen to me. I know that you don't care, but you know the company's policy. I will lose my job."

"So, you can find another one. I'm not worth your job?" she asked, and he couldn't believe that she would ask such an oblivious question. He ignored it and said that it was time for them to leave. He immediately called for the check and paid for a dinner they never received in order to get the hell out of Dodge.

The waitress didn't know what was going on and asked if they would like their food to go. Leon declined and left a gratuity. He asked the waitress if there was a back exit, and she gladly led the way through the back door after receiving a hundred-dollar tip.

Amber complained the entire time he was making their grand escape and Leon wanted to put some tape over her mouth. He didn't want to hear it, and it wasn't the time or place.

The parking attendant took their ticket and within five minutes Leon's car was retrieved. They got inside the car and as soon as the doors closed, Amber shouted, "You are such a wussy."

"Well, you sure didn't mind me being a wussy the other night. I wasn't a wussy then, huh?"

"Whatever. You're acting like I'm a child. I'm not a child. My grandparents don't run my life and they won't tell me who I can or cannot date."

Leon wanted to get her to relax because what he had to tell her was going to send her even more over the top. He pulled into an empty parking lot and that's where he told her that he could no longer see her. It wasn't worth risking and losing his job. Amber went ballistic and didn't let him finish. She began hitting him and yelling. He tried to shield his face and held her arms tight, begging her to stop hitting him and to talk like *adults*. She wouldn't listen. She began screaming and trying to hit him with her shoe. He kept trying to get her to calm down, but she wouldn't. He wanted to take her home and be done with her, but instead, she got out of the car crying, her mascara running the same race as her tears. She limped with one shoe on and one shoe off, screaming, "Fuck you, Leon Knight. I hate you." He got out of the car and tried to comfort her, but she continued.

"Amber, let me take you home."

"Fuck you. I don't want you taking me nowhere."

"Amber, please. Stop making a scene." She limped off, holding one stiletto in one hand and the other on her foot, crying and signaling for a cab. Refusing any of his pleas to calm down and take her home.

"Fuck you, Leon."

Leon was shaken when he pulled into his driveway. He noticed Kurt's car outside and felt a sigh of relief that Barbara's wasn't alone. She was in the kitchen with books everywhere on the table and Kurt was there studying with her. Barbara heard the door unlock and saw her dad disheveled like he had been in a fight.

"Hey Dad, are you okay?" she asked with concern.

"Yeah, Mr. Knight. It looks like you've been in a fight," Kurt blurted. Barbara looked at him and her eyes said it all: *mind yo' business.*

"I'm fine. You too go ahead with your studying. I'm going upstairs to take a shower and relax."

"Dad, are you sure you're okay? You don't look good."

"I'm just tired. I had a long night."

"Well, if you need to talk, I'm here for you. There's some veggie and supreme pizza in the oven if you are hungry."

"Thanks, Pumpkin." He squeezed Barbara's arm to let her know that he was okay as he went upstairs to take a shower and try to get his mind together. He didn't know if Amber arrived home safely or if he still had a job to go to in the morning.

He turned on the TV to watch the local news because he was worried about Amber. He called her but she didn't answer. His calls went straight to voicemail. He didn't know what to do, so he continued watching when **"Breaking News"** flashed across the screen.

An unidentified woman was struck by a car tonight while exiting a vehicle. Security cameras caught this vehicle leaving the scene moments before the woman was hit. Her condition is unknown. If you have any information, please contact the local police department.

Leon watched as his car left the scene. He also noticed Amber's cream-colored stiletto lying in the street.

"Oh my God. What have I done?" Leon said. He began sobbing and Barbara rushed upstairs to see what was wrong. He was shaking when she entered the room.

"Dad, Dad, what's wrong?"

Leon couldn't speak. He pointed to the TV but there wasn't anything there but a McDonald's commercial. He changed the channel to see if the incident was on another broadcast station and it was on KENS. Barbara saw her father's car and began to cry. "Dad, what happened? What did you do?" Barbara kept asking while watching the news report.

Kurt ran upstairs when he heard Barbara wailing. He stood there in a trance. He didn't know what to do. He began watching the TV to figure out what was wrong with them.

"Dad, what happened?" Barbara kept asking but she got no response.

"Yeah, what happened Mr. Knight? That looks like your car?" Leon dried his tears and began telling Barbara and Kurt what happened. He started from the beginning and didn't leave any details out. Barbara insisted that they needed to go to the police and explain everything that he just told them. Leon agreed with his daughter, and she and Kurt left the bedroom while he got dressed. Kurt offered to take him because he was in no condition to drive.

They arrived at the police station and asked to speak with someone regarding the accident that had occurred a few hours earlier, with the unidentified woman struck by the car. The chief of police was called in to speak with Leon. Kurt and Barbara waited in the lobby as she sobbed into his arms. Kurt held her tight, like he was never letting her go, running his fingers through her flatiron coils trying to comfort her. She apologized for bringing him into her family's ordeal because she knew they both had an exam the next day. She was in no condition to go to school let alone take an exam. Barbara drifted off to sleep and was awakened by her father's voice telling her that it was time to go home. She asked about the conversation with the chief of police and he said he needed to stay close and not leave town in case they had any further questions for him. He'd given them Amber's full name and they were going to contact her next of kin. Leon said that he asked about her condition, but the Chief couldn't release that information since he was not related. He didn't know what hospital she was taken to, and he didn't ask. He was still under investigation.

Kurt dropped Barbara and her dad at home and offered to stay with her a little bit longer until she fell asleep, but she wanted him to go home and get some rest and not worry about her. She would be fine now that her father had gone to the precinct to explain his side of the story. She wished Kurt a good-night and he said he would be there in the morning to pick her up for school.

Barbara took her shower and quickly drifted into a deep slumber. Her phone displayed twelve text message notifications, but she ignored them all. She wanted this nightmare of a night to go away.

Leon retired to his room and phoned every nearby hospital trying to find out if they had an Amber McNeil, and if so, what her condition was. He knew if Amber passed away that he would never forgive himself, and the loss of his job would be the least of his worries. He wanted to call in sick in the morning but thought it might alarm his coworkers if neither he or Amber were at work, since they hardly ever called in. He decided that he would go to work, with the hopes of not raising any suspicions.

Billy was standing at Sasha's locker talking and laughing with her when he saw Barbara and Kurt coming down the hallway. He and Sasha noticed that Barbara didn't look too good. It looked like she had been crying all night. Billy immediately thought that Kurt had done something to her, and if so, he was going to handle it man to man. But as they got closer and Sasha asked her cousin what was wrong, Barbara burst into tears. She pulled Sasha to the side and told her what happened with her father. Sasha comforted her, telling her everything would work out and how it wasn't his fault.

While Barbara and Sasha stood aside talking, Billy mean mugged Kurt. Kurt ignored him because he wasn't in the mood for "Bill's" attitude. And before Billy could ask, Kurt blurted out, "Hey man, I had nothing to do with it. It's not even about me." Billy wasn't buying it until Sasha and Barbara returned and it appeared that she felt a little better. Kurt placed his arm around her, and she didn't resist, which convinced Billy her tears were because of something else. Billy pulled his claws in, but he'd been ready to attack Kurt if he had done anything to hurt her.

"Babe, are you okay?" Sasha asked Billy.

"Yeah, I'm fine, but what was that all about?"

"I'll tell you later. But we have to get to class," she said as Billy walked her to English and then left to go to his. He kept thinking about Barbara and wanted to know what was wrong with her. He didn't want to wait until Sasha told him. He wanted to know now.

He sat in class, pulled out his phone, and sent her a text.

"Hey, r u all right? Did Jheri Curl Kurt do something to you?"

When Barbara pulled out her phone and read Billy's message she couldn't help but laugh.

"After reading your text I feel much better. :-) :-) :-) :-)"

She ended her text with all kinds of emojis. Billy didn't know whether she accidentally or intentionally sent them, but he didn't ask. His only concern was that she was okay. He put his phone back into his jacket and smiled since she'd at least responded to his text this time. She hadn't the night before. He wanted to make sure that their *friendship* was still intact before he broke the news that he and Sasha were a couple.

Chapter Eleven

Leon arrived at work trying to look as normal as possible. He checked Amber's office to see if she was there, even though he knew she wouldn't be. It was wishful thinking. The space was empty and felt melancholy in her absence. He said a silent prayer for the two of them as he walked past the breakroom. He hadn't eaten anything all day or night since the incident, nor did he have any appetite. He needed and wanted to know the condition of his former lover.

He heard a noise in the distance coming from the elevator, the ping of it as the doors opened and closed, but he saw no one. Leon walked abruptly to his office trying to concentrate, to no avail. It was almost lunch time when he decided enough was enough and he would leave for the day. On his way out, he noticed a group of coworkers whispering. When he walked toward them they all began working. He felt his colleagues' stares burn through the interior and exterior of his soul. He quickly pushed the elevator down arrow and when the doors opened he headed to the lower-level parking garage. As he exited the elevator he saw Rebecca returning from her lunch break.

"Where you rushing off to?" Rebecca asked.

"I'm feeling a little sick so I'm just going to try and sleep it off."

"Oh, where's Ms. Amber? I haven't seen her all day."

"I'm not sure. Why are you asking me?"

"I just asked. That's all. So when can you and I go out for lunch?"

Leon couldn't believe Rebecca was trying to get next to him. It wasn't that he felt she was beneath him but she reminded him of his mother. He wanted to put it to her nicely, but then again, maybe she was the reason he was in this position with Amber. If he would have put Amber in her place from the beginning, then he wouldn't be checking every news channel trying to find updates on her condition.

"Ms. Rebecca, with all due respect, I don't want to have lunch with you. I'm not interested in a relationship. Now, if you would excuse me, I would like to go home."

Rebecca grabbed her chest in disbelief and told him that she only wanted to be his friend because of what a nice guy he was, but she wasn't interested in him romantically. They both laughed at themselves for thinking the worst, only to find that needed companionship was being offered.

"In that case, I will take a rain check."

She accepted and wished him well.

If Rebecca didn't know anything about Amber, maybe he was just imagining his coworkers gossiping about him. Rebecca was eyewitness news and if she hadn't heard about the accident then the others wouldn't have either. But he knew it would be soon and waited for his fate.

Leon got home and fixed himself some tea with lemon and a little shot of whiskey. He wrapped himself under his blanket and turned on the TV to search for any updates on Amber. He called her phone but still got no answer. He didn't leave any messages because he didn't want to be caught if someone had her phone. There were no updates on the news, so he flipped through the channels to watch a movie. His phone rang and it was Mr. Thomas from the dealership confirming that his car would be delivered on Friday. He had been so caught up with the incident that he completely forgot about his daughter's eighteenth birthday.

"Yes, sir. I will be home to accept it. Thank you so much," Leon said. When he ended the call, a text message came in from an unknown number.

"She will be eighteen, it's time for her to know the truth. J.W."

He didn't have the time or energy to deal with the truth. He needed to find out Amber's status and get his daughter's surprise gift. He kept flipping channels and phoning local hospitals until he finally called Methodist Hospital and learned she had been admitted there but they couldn't release her status. Leon sighed and wondered if he could go to the hospital unnoticed, but instead he went downstairs to try and force himself to eat. He came back and got in bed with a hoagie sandwich and a bag of Lay's potato chips.

An hour later, he was fast asleep when Barbara came home to check on him. She wasn't sure whether to wake him or not, so she went into the kitchen and ate some leftover vegetable pizza before retiring to her room. She tried to study but she couldn't help thinking about all the events that had occurred, starting with the unidentified caller asking to see her. She still hadn't fully discussed it with her father but ever since the incident with Amber, she didn't know when the talk would happen.

The doorbell rang and Barbara went to answer it, but there was no one there. She looked around and saw Mrs. Hopkins, who greeted her, but Barbara didn't ask if she saw anyone. Barbara quickly closed and locked the door. Instead of going back to her room, she decided to study at the kitchen table. Her father came downstairs dressed and looking much better. He was on his way to the hospital but didn't want Barbara to know. He told her that he was going to the store and asked if she needed anything, but she didn't. As he was going out the front door, he found Sasha and Billy about to ring the doorbell.

"Uncle. How are you?" Sasha asked as she hugged him tight. She didn't want to let go. She told him she was sorry about what he was going through and that she was praying everything would be okay. He accepted her embrace and figured Barbara had told her about Amber. He thanked her and greeted Billy before he left for the store.

"Hey cousin, we came by to see if you wanted to go and get something to eat?"

"Can I take a rain check?"

"No, not this time. You can't over study and besides you need to clear your mind. Give it a rest." Billy agreed and tried to help Barbara feel better, but he saw the anxiety written all over her face. She looked at the amount of studying she had to do and pointed out she'd just had leftover pizza and really wasn't hungry. But Sasha was insistent, and decided to order Chinese food because she didn't want Barbara to be alone.

Sasha popped in a DVD and she and Billy began watching an old classic movie, *Cooley High.* The distractions were too much for Barbara, so she sat down in her dad's La-Z-Boy chair and began watching the movie with them. The doorbell rang and it was the Chinese food delivery. Billy paid, and they began eating their food. He'd ordered Barbara fried rice with vegetables and cream cheese rangoons in case she got hungry later. He and Sasha ate teriyaki and lemon pepper chicken with fried noodles. After eating, Sasha cleaned up and put the leftovers in the refrigerator. She sat down next to Billy, grabbed his hand, and held it tight. He looked into her eyes and knew he was with the girl who he wanted to spend the rest of his life with. Barbara looked at them and saw that they were happy. She was elated for them.

Barbara heard her phone ring and it was Kurt asking if she needed any help studying. She accepted and invited him over.

Kurt arrived and Barbara let him in. She asked if he was hungry and offered him leftover pizza or Chinese food. He opted for the leftover pizza and Billy was glad because he didn't want to be petty, but he hadn't bought food for Kurt.

"Oh cool, *Cooley High.* Man, this is my all-time favorite movie," Kurt said as he sat next to Sasha. Billy squeezed his arm around her even tighter. He began reciting all the dialogue in the movie and Billy immediately stopped him.

"Man, can you just watch the movie?"

"Ooh, yeah. Sorry." Kurt then began questioning Billy and Sasha's relationship, and Billy seemed annoyed, but he was kind of glad because he didn't know how to tell Barbara that they were official. He and Sasha confirmed that they were exclusive.

"Congratulations. It's the way it's supposed to be; the star quarterback and the head cheerleader." Barbara cleared her throat, congratulated them both, and agreed with Kurt that they made a *cute* couple. Billy noticed Barbara's insincere tone and wished that he had told her in private. But he wanted to make sure that he and Barbara were still cool and could occasionally hang out. He felt silly wondering if it would be okay with Sasha or even if Barbara would agree to it.

"So, y'all gone get married after high school?" Kurt's outspoken and nosy self wanted to know. Sasha looked at Billy and waited for him to answer, but Barbara interrupted and told Kurt to mind his business. He did what he was told and went into the kitchen to get another Coke. He asked if anyone else wanted one and they all declined.

It had been over two hours and the movie had ended but Leon still wasn't back from the store. Barbara decided to go into the other room and phone him while Sasha put on another movie. She kept getting his voicemail, which was unusual since her dad *always* answered when she called. Sasha went to check on Barbara since she hadn't come back into the living room. She saw her on her phone and looked worried.

"Hey Barbara, is everything okay?"

"Yeah, it's just that I haven't heard from my dad. He said that he was just going to the store, but he's not answering his phone."

Sasha assured her that he was fine and suggested he'd gone to clear his mind with everything happening. Barbara thought she would send herself into an early grave if she kept worrying so much and agreed with Sasha. They went to continue watching the movie. Barbara was getting sleepy and tired and it was getting late. Kurt decided to call it a night but Sasha wanted to stay with Barbara until her uncle came home. Billy didn't want to leave either of them alone and offered to stay with them and leave as soon as they heard from Leon. He could sleep on the couch. Barbara retrieved a blanket from the closet and gave it to him. She walked Kurt to the front door and he leaned in and tried to kiss her. She opted for a warm hug instead. He left feeling like a little lost puppy but understood that she was going through a lot with her father.

Billy saw the interaction and smiled, thinking Kurt was just shot down like a dog in the street. Well, not that harsh, but close. Sasha stood behind him watching Kurt and Barbara. She noticed Billy smile and wondered what that was all about. Barbara closed the door as soon as she saw Kurt get into his car and drive off. She looked around to see if her dad was coming down the street, but no such luck. She closed and locked the door and asked if Billy and Sasha needed anything before she went to take her shower. Sasha told her that she would be up to check on her later. She waited until Barbara left and decided to ask Billy about her cousin.

"Billy, can I ask you a question? But you have to promise not to get offended." He pulled Sasha close and told her to ask him anything as he nibbled on her ear. To his surprise, she asked if he liked her cousin.

"Why would you ask me something like that when I got you? Barbara and I are just *friends*. Babe, come on..." She stopped him from grabbing her and then told him that she would be upstairs.

"And what's that supposed to mean?" he called out, but she kept walking like he didn't exist. She didn't believe him.

She entered Barbara's bedroom and looked at all the decor. She hadn't been in her room since last year. She knew her cousin was a nerd but this was too much. Her room was decorated with NASA and outer space themes. She didn't know whether she loved or hated it since it wasn't girly-girl like her room. She saw the football that Billy had given her too.

Barbara came out of the restroom and saw Sasha looking at her books and surveying her room.

"Hey cousin, I thought you were downstairs with Billy."

"No, he's a big boy and besides I wanted to ask you something about him."

"Yeah, what is it?"

Barbara's cell phone rang as she told Sasha to hold that thought. She answered immediately.

"Hello?"

"This is Methodist Hospital; may I please speak with Mrs. Knight?"

"Yes, this is she."

A female voice spoke softly as she delivered the horrifying news. Barbara dropped her phone and began crying. She needed to get to the hospital immediately.

"Cousin, what is it?"

"My dad has been in an accident. I got to call Aunt Suzie."

After her phone call to Aunt Suzie, Barbara got dressed, and she, Sasha, and Billy were on their way to the hospital. They met up with Suzie at the nurse's station trying to get information about Leon. The nurse told them to wait in the visitor's room for a doctor to update them on his status.

Dr. Ibo entered the room asking to speak with Suzie and explained that her brother needed a blood transfusion due to the loss of blood. He had been in a bad car accident. Suzie was in no condition to give blood, she was on Coumadin, a blood thinner, and couldn't afford to donate. She asked if Barbara and Sasha could donate and the doctor said that would be fine, so the nurse took Barbara and Sasha back to the room to draw blood. The nurse pricked Sasha's finger first and read the results.

"Perfect, you have the same blood type," she said. Then she pricked Barbara's finger. When she saw the result, she reread both with concern and asked which one of them was Leon's daughter. Barbara said, "I'm his daughter." The nurse looked at Barbara's blood results for the third time. She told Barbara that she wouldn't be able to use her blood because it didn't match her father's, but Sasha's blood matched.

"What do you mean, you can't use my blood? He's my father. Barbara cried out."

"Ms. Knight, please calm down. There must be a mistake. Leon couldn't possibly be your father." Barbara ran down the hallway into the waiting room, looked at her auntie, and told her what the nurse said. Suzie held Barbara in her arms trying to calm her down.

"Auntie, how is it that my blood doesn't match my father's but Sasha's does?"

Aunt Suzie didn't know how to answer or whether it was her place. Barbara continued to sob and Billy stood there helpless and watched. He wanted to wrap her tight in his arms and let her know that everything was going to be okay, that he got her. He hesitated but couldn't let Barbara suffer in so much pain without comforting her, so he held her. But as soon as he did, Sasha came around the corner and watched her cousin crying into her man's arms.

Chapter Twelve

Barbara sat at her father's bedside as she had for the past six months, holding his hand, examining all the symmetrical features of his face, hands, and all body parts down to his pinky toes. She wanted to know who this man was who had raised her for eighteen years. A man who had a Toyota Corolla delivered to her for her birthday that she never got to celebrate. She could only cry in Kurt, Sasha, Aunt Suzie, and Billy's arms. She cried to whomever was available and would listen. It wasn't how her eighteenth birthday was supposed to be and she continued to pray that her father would come out of his long six-month coma soon.

It had been a lot on her with school, traveling to see him, and taking care of their home. She had graduated high school and was enrolled at Howard University on a full scholarship. Leon had invested and saved well, so Barbara was able to keep the home afloat and was thankful that the mortgage was paid in full since the home was passed down from Leon's parents. He had long-term disability and insurance that covered his medical bills. He'd also saved for Barbara's college fund since the day she was born, which she was now living off of. She admired her father's financial planning, but she didn't know him. He was a mystery outside of being the loving father she has always known.

She opened her purse to pull out the police investigation report to re-read how the accident occurred. Tears rolled down her golden-brown cheeks as she kissed her father's hands and asked,

"Why? Why would you try and kill yourself, Dad? You are all that I have."

"You got me, cousin." Sasha walked into the hospital room with her mother, Elizabeth. She had seen and heard Barbara talking to her dad. She put her arms around her and squeezed her tight. She wanted to know when Barbara got into town and welcomed her to the guest room at her home because she didn't want Barbara to be alone. Barbara didn't mind the alone time. But she still didn't understand how her blood type didn't match her father's and her cousin was able to give blood to save his life. She needed answers and everyone including her Aunt Suzie was tight lipped. Suzie knew Leon was harboring a secret and didn't want to get involved because it wasn't her place.

"Barbara, honey, you need some rest. Why don't you and Sasha go home and I will be there later to cook you a nice warm meal. You look terrible." Lizzy tried to convince her that it would be better for her health. Sasha agreed with her mother and practically picked Barbara out of the chair and began walking her out of the door. Barbara had no choice but to leave with her.

"Sasha, I will be home soon. Barbara, I will stay here with your father until then."

"Thanks, Mom."

"Thank you, Aunt Lizzy."

As soon as Barbara and Sasha were out of sight, Lizzy reached over to give Leon a kiss on his cheek. And then she began chastising him as if he was a child, telling him that he needed to get his butt out of that bed. He was too young to be sleeping for so many months. She compared him to Rip Van Winkle.

"You're still the same bitch." a familiar voice spoke from a distance. Elizabeth turned toward the door and couldn't believe her eyes. She hadn't seen her in over ten years but there she stood looking young, vibrant, and just like her daughter.

"Jenny, what are you doing here?"

"What do you mean, what am *I* doing here? The question *is*, what are you doing here?"

"You still got that bitterness in you, huh? You still haven't gotten over it?"

"Yeah, once a whore is always a whore."

Aunt Suzie tapped on the door, saw the exchange between the two siblings, and knew that she had come at the right time.

Elizabeth and Jenny were only eleven months apart, but looked just like twins, and had been at each other's throats from the first time she met them. She was the one who introduced her brother to Jenny. It was love at first sight, but then Leon and Jenny got into a big fight, and broke up, that's when all hell broke loose. Leon and Jenny were keeping secrets, but Jenny wasn't aware of what came of the affair until ten years later. That's when she left and found her a younger man. Today was the first day that anyone had heard from her, and it appeared that she was back to wreak havoc.

"Oh, would you two be quiet. I'm trying to sleep."

Suzie walked between the two sisters and grabbed her brother and cried, "Leon, Leon, oh my God. My brother just spoke. What did you say again?" She wanted to make sure her eyes and ears weren't playing tricks on her.

"I said that I'm trying to get some rest."

Suzie hugged him and kept saying that she was glad he was back. She told Lizzy to go and get the doctor, that her brother was back. Lizzy did as she was told, and the nurse entered the room before Dr. Ibo. She took his vitals while the doctor shined a light to examine his eyes.

"Get that damn light out of my face," Leon fussed. Everyone in the room laughed because he had never been a grumpy man, but coming out of his coma made him one. They didn't care, they were all happy that he was back.

Dr. Ibo continued his examination regardless of Leon not wanting to be touched. He wanted to sleep in peace, not knowing that he had been asleep for six months. He'd missed his daughter's high school graduation and the news that Amber had fully recovered from her injuries but had suffered from amnesia. She didn't remember anything that happened that night, or her and Leon's affair. So, when he recovered, he still had a job to return to if he so desired.

Leon tried to sit up, but the nurse told him to take it easy. He wanted to make sure that the woman he once loved was standing next to him. The nurse and Dr. Ibo left the room, saying they would be back later. He ordered the nurse to get Leon plenty of fluids and change the IV bag.

"Jenny, is that you?"

"Yeah, it's me." She shrugged like she wasn't happy that he had come out of his coma.

"What are you doing here?"

"I come to tell *my* daughter the truth."

"Mama, is that you? Tell me the truth about what?" Barbara asked as she walked in the door. She and Sasha got all the way home before she realized that she had left her phone on top of the AC vent when she was looking out the window and they'd come back to the hospital to retrieve it. Sasha stood behind her staring at her aunt Jenny who she hadn't seen since she was a little girl.

"Yes, it's your mother, baby." She grabbed her daughter and didn't want to let go. She wanted her to know everything, and now that she was eighteen, she figured it was time. Leon tried to object but Jenny was persistent and didn't want to hear anything he had to say. She held her daughter close and rubbed her fingers through her 4a textured hair. She began to speak but Leon kept interrupting. Barbara begged her dad to let her mother go on.

"Dad, can you please let her talk? I want to know the truth."

Lizzy interrupted her, which made Jenny even more upset. She told her that she needed to let her daughter in on her *little secret* as well. And Sasha thought to herself, *wait a minute what does this have to do with me?"*

Suzie tried her best to mediate the situation, afraid they would be asked to leave the hospital. But Jenny wouldn't stop until her man Hakeem walked into the room and took her outside. Barbara followed her mother like a child being abandoned. Leon tried to get out of the bed to tell Jenny that that was enough but fell to the floor and hit his head. The nurse rushed in to see what the ruckus was about, saw Leon lying there unconscious, and asked everyone to leave the room immediately as she called for Dr. Ibo.

The nurse and male orderly rushed to help Leon to his feet and back into the bed. Dr. Ibo came to examine him. Barbara tried to enter the room but was not allowed inside. She cried into her mother's arms as she held her tight. She, her mother, Suzie, Sasha, and Elizabeth walked into the wait area to hear any information on Leon's fall. They put their differences aside and prayed. Suzie led the way with tears in her eyes trying to hold it together so that Barbara didn't get more emotional than she already was. After praying, they sat there and watched each other. No one wanted to take the blame for what happened, but Lizzy blamed Jenny for coming back after ten years and upsetting Barbara and Leon. She wouldn't dare voice her thoughts because she wanted peace until she heard back from the doctor.

"He's going to be okay, cousin," Sasha said as she rubbed Barbara's back, comforting her. Barbara turned to embrace Sasha.

"Thank you, Sasha. Thanks for all your support."

Dr. Ibo walked into the waiting area wanting to know what all the commotion was about. Since Leon had just awakened from a coma, he didn't need the stress due to health concerns. He announced that he suffered a concussion but was stable and would be all right. Dr. Ibo was restricting visitors for the day but they could come back tomorrow. He wanted to continue to monitor Leon without all the distractions.

"Doctor, can I please see him? I want to see my father," Barbara pleaded.

"I'm sorry. I can't. You and your family are going to have to come back tomorrow," Dr. Ibo said, not waiting for them to respond. He meant what he said, and he was on to his next patient.

Jenny was the first to ask why he had to be so snob? She kept going on and on about his appearance. Hakeem tried to calm her, to no avail. She was clearly upset about the doctor's decision and so was everyone else but they decided to be humble.

It was time for everyone to leave, and Barbara wanted to spend more time with her mother, so she told Sasha that she would be over later in the night. Sasha didn't appear to be upset, even though she wanted to hang out with Barbara and talk about her long-distance relationship with Billy. She felt that he was seeing someone else because every time she called him, he was either studying, watching films, or practicing. He didn't have much time for her and it was weighing on her emotionally.

Billy earned a full scholarship to the University of Texas in Austin and Sasha was attending St. Mary's University to become an attorney. She didn't want to leave home so when St. Mary's offered her a full scholarship, she couldn't accept it fast enough. But being away from Billy was stressing her out, and her grades were paying the price. She and Billy had planned to spend spring break together but he hadn't mentioned it in over a month. Sasha thought about how whenever her cousin got the opportunity, she would come from Washington, DC to visit. She knew she had to check on her father, but it was a lot further away than UT in Austin and she felt that Billy wasn't putting in the effort to come home.

Barbara's tears brought Sasha back from her self-pity party as she hugged her. She was too emotional, and it was best for her to stay with her mom, who she hadn't seen in ten years. They had a lot of catching up to do and Barbara had so many unanswered questions.

"Aunt Jenny, it was good seeing you, and nice to meet you, Hakeem," Sasha said as she and everyone else walked to their cars.

"Maybe we can get together soon. You, me, and Barbara, and have a girls' day out," Jenny offered.

"I would love to. Just let me know when," Sasha said, and bid them goodnight before she left.

Barbara greeted Aunt Suzie, saw that she made it to her car safely, and her mother followed her home. When Sasha and Elizabeth got home, they began discussing everything that had taken place. Sasha asked about her mother's relationship with Jenny but Elizabeth was too exhausted to talk about it. She decided to grab some leftover fettuccine from the refrigerator and call it a night.

Jimmy arrived home a few hours later and wanted to know Leon's status but Elizabeth didn't have an answer. She filled him in on Jenny and the events that had taken place. He was shocked that Jenny was in town. He knew about the toxic sibling relationship between his wife and her sister. He asked how long she would be in town but Elizabeth didn't know. The only thing she wanted to know was when she was leaving. Jenny knew too many secrets and Lizzy was concerned about them being exposed to Barbara and Sasha before she got the opportunity to explain. She decided that she would call Jenny the next day to make a peace offering, discuss why she was in town after all these years, and what brought her back to San Antonio.

Jenny dropped Hakeem off at the hotel and she and Barbara went to get something to eat so they'd have time to talk. But before getting to the eatery, Barbara let her know she was vegetarian. "Vegetarian? How did that come about?" Jenny began questioning her about the reasons and explaining that she was a meat woman and needed her meat and potatoes. She went on and on about different dishes that *required* meat. Barbara wanted to hear why she'd left her, but her diet preference was the focus of their conversation. Jenny wanted to know if she was dating anyone and Barbara mentioned a guy from college. She wanted to hear all about him. After they got something to eat, Barbara asked how long Jenny was in town and her mother mentioned that she was moving back home and looking for a house. Barbara was elated. She couldn't wait to get to know her mother better and tell her how much she missed her. Barbara asked to be dropped off at Sasha's home and suggested they have their girls' day out the next day before she flew back to Washington on Sunday for school. She wished that she could stay longer, but she had exams and wanted to graduate on time. Jenny agreed and said that she would pick them up at noon.

They arrived at Sasha's and as soon as they bid their farewells, Barbara received a text message from her father letting her know that he was fine and would be released from the hospital soon. He wanted to call her but didn't want to upset her more than she already was when he last saw her. She texted him back that she would see him the next day.

"Goodnight, Pumpkin. I love you."

"Love you too, Dad."

Barbara called Sasha on her cell phone to let her know she was at the front door. She didn't want to wake her aunt and uncle. Within seconds, she opened the door. Barbara told Sasha that she was exhausted but she'd heard from her father, who would be released from the hospital soon. Sasha was relieved to hear it, and the girls' day out was planned for the next day at noon. Barbara's mother would pick them up.

Sasha took Barbara to the guest room and gave her some sleepwear. She wanted to talk to her about Billy but knew she had a lot more going on with her father *and* mother, and she didn't want to cause any more problems.

"Thank you, cousin, I really appreciate all that you have done."

"Barb, I'm your cousin and that's what we are for. And besides, you are like my baby sister." She and Barbara were a month apart in age. "I will see you in the morning. If you need anything let me know," Sasha insisted before retiring to bed.

Barbara slept only an hour before she was awakened by a car engine. She looked outside the window, saw her uncle leaving, and wondered where he was going at that time of the night. She closed the curtains and decided to watch television but there wasn't anything that interested her. She began reading, and within minutes, she was fast asleep.

Chapter Thirteen

Billy sat in the weight room icing his sore arm and shoulder. He had to get some help on the offensive line or he wouldn't make it to the NFL. High school was different from college, and he was having trouble adapting. He missed his mother and sister, and even though he talked to them regularly, he hadn't had any time to go home and visit. He knew that Sasha was feeling neglected, and that wasn't his intent, but his schedule was overwhelmingly busy. He promised his mother that he would finish college before entering the pros, so he took his classwork more seriously. The only consolation he had was that Wilt was attending UT in Austin and helped with his homesickness.

"Hey man, how long are you going to be a baby and stay icing up?"

"If you took as many hits as I've taken, you'd be crying like one," Billy teased.

"Whatever, I ain't no baby. But anyway, you know Alpha Phi Alpha is having a party so let's go check out the honeys." Wilt said with excitement.

"Naw, I'm not interested. I got my 'honey' back home and I ain't about to lose her messing around with your blowup-doll ass. How is Zula anyway?"

"Aww, you got jokes, huh? Forget you then, I'll go by myself. Besides, I don't need you honey blocking like you did in high school." Billy couldn't believe his ears. He had never done such a thing. Besides, Wilt thought he didn't know about him and Olivia. Brandy had filled him in on their secret affair, but Billy kept that to himself and was waiting for Wilt to tell him. It had been over six months and he hadn't even mentioned her.

"Well, I'm going to holla at you later but if you change your mind. It's at Jester's residence hall."

"Have fun," Billy said as he threw up the peace sign. He didn't have time for parties, in fact, he needed to call and check on his girl as soon as he was done.

Thirty minutes later he was showered and walking back to his dorm when he saw Brooke pass by him. He spoke to her, and she smiled. She reminded him of Barbara, and if he hadn't been with Sasha, he would be trying to get with her. He wasn't a player, he was a one-woman man and could never disrespect Sasha by cheating on her. Brooke stumbled and dropped her economics book. Billy picked it up and made sure that she was okay as she thanked him.

"Are you sure, you don't need me to carry you wherever you're going? I don't want you falling and hurting yourself."

She laughed and assured him that she was fine. It was Billy that made her nervous because she'd had a crush on him ever since the start of the semester. He was gorgeous, respectful, and a gentleman. She never saw him talking to any girls and knew he wasn't a player, but what she didn't know was that he had a girlfriend back home in San Antonio.

The phone rang as soon as Billy entered his dorm and Wilt answered after the first ring. It was Sasha needing to talk to Billy, but he wondered why she didn't call on his cell phone instead of the dorm landline. Billy took the phone out of Wilt's hand as he finished getting dressed for the party.

"Hey babe, how are you?" Sasha began telling him about her day and how her Aunt Jenny was back in town, and her uncle was recovering from his accident. She began talking about their relationship and how she felt neglected and wondered if there was someone else.

"Babe, you know there is no one else, and you know how much I love you. Don't even go there." He continued assuring her that there was no one, that his schedule had been hectic, and he promised to be there for spring break. He asked her about school, and she didn't want to tell him that her grades were suffering because she was missing him, so she lied and said everything was all good and she was on track to graduate on time. Before they ended their conversation, he asked about Barbara. She told him she was staying in the guestroom and would be returning to Washington on Sunday, but they were having a girls' day out the next day with Barbara's mother. He told her to say hello to his *friend* and she obliged.

"Have a good night, babe, and I love you."

"You too, and ditto. I will call you tomorrow."

"You better." Sasha reprimanded. Billy laughed because she was still that spicy little cheerleader that he had fallen in love with. When Billy hung up the phone, Wilt was still there in his ear begging him to go to the party.

"Man, just go for thirty minutes and if it's whack, we will both be out."

Billy sighed and said, "Look, ten minutes and then we are out."

"Fifteen tops," Wilt said, and Billy agreed. He was dressed and they were on their way to the party soon after.

They entered the hall, and the party was jumpin'. Not only with music, but it seemed like the women outnumbered the men, and they were all brick houses.

"DAMN," Billy said out loud.

"Didn't I tell you it was going to be dope?" Wilt said as he bobbed his head to the music, holding his left hand in a position cuffed to his mouth, and his right hand between his pants legs like he needed to go to the bathroom. It didn't take Billy long to notice a group of women, and Brooke sitting there talking with them. He wondered what she was doing there and thought maybe she did have more freak in her than he thought. He walked toward her, and Wilt was on his trail asking where he was going,

"Hey Brooke, I didn't know you would be here."

"Me either. My girls asked me to come for a little while and said if I didn't like it I could leave." Wilt laughed because it was the same pact that he and Billy had made. He nudged Billy and cleared his throat for an introduction.

"Oh, Brooke, this is my man, Wilt. Wilt, this is Brooke." Wilt grabbed Brooke's hand and proceeded to kiss it. Billy thought, this was the reason he couldn't go anywhere with Wilt. He didn't even know her and there he was kissing her hand. Brooke didn't seem to mind. In fact, she was flattered.

"Nice to meet you," they both said in unison. Brooke began introducing her friends, and everyone exchanged pleasantries by waving or nodding their heads. The lights dimmed and Luther Vandross's, "If This World Were Mine" blared through the speakers. Wilt asked Brooke if she would like to dance, and she accepted. They walked to the center of the room where the other students were slow dancing and joined them. Billy stood and watched as they danced for three more songs. He checked his phone, saw that it was getting late, and when Wilt and Brooke took a break from the dance floor, he asked if Wilt was ready to go. Wilt told him to go ahead, that he was staying because he enjoyed Brooke's presence. He whispered to Billy:

"It looks like I won't be needing my blowup doll Zula anymore." He and Billy laughed. Brooke wanted to know what they were laughing about but decided to ignore it. Billy left and Wilt continued to accompany Brooke.

Hours later, Wilt returned to the dorm to wake Billy and said he thought he was in love.

Billy slept in while Wilt met Brooke for an early-morning breakfast. Afterward, they watched a matinee at the nearby movie theater. Their connection was moving way too fast. He'd just met her last night, but it seemed like they had been together in another world. He held her close and inhaled her scent, and admired every second of her light brown eyes and chestnut complexion. Her natural coils were tied in a pink floral headwrap that matched her sweat suit. Wilt towered over her, but she didn't mind. His strong arms made her feel like a natural woman. He was her *first* love interest because her Baptist parents hadn't allowed her to even look at boys.

Wilt didn't have parents to speak of. He was an orphan, adopted by his grandmother. His mother was still on drugs and his father was in prison for armed robbery and murder, so he considered himself an orphan. Wilt's grandmother, Sadie, promised to raise him nothing like his parents. She didn't know what went wrong with her daughter, Erika. She knew Wilt Sr. was no good the moment her daughter introduced him. He was a high school prospect in football but decided that hustling was more important, and from then on he got involved with drugs and took Erika down the same path. She was pregnant with Wilt before she began her drug tour, and thank God he was born before her addiction. Wilt had a sister, but she was stillborn and the heartbreak of losing her daughter took his mother to the deep end. She never recovered.

"Hey Wilt, are you okay?" Brooke asked.

"Everything is perfect. In fact, what are you doing for the rest of your life?"

"W-what?" Brooke stammered.

"Are you asking me for my hand in marriage?" she asked.

"Naw, I'm asking you to be my lady." Brooke felt embarrassed and thought *what a stupid question*. They had just met last night, why would he ask her to be his wife? She thought about it for a second before answering. She wanted to give him a little taste of his own medicine.

He asked, "Is that a yes?"

She thought about it a little bit more and whispered in his ear, "Only if you meet my parents."

"Right, right, I'm up for it. But when?"

"They are coming to visit tomorrow."

"Tomorrow?" Wilt was surprised to meet them so soon.

"Yes, is there a problem?"

He put on his Mack Daddy confidence and pretended as though he wasn't nervous about meeting her parents. "No, I'm ready to meet them."

She was elated and began telling him all about them, though what she revealed made him even more nervous. He had to put on his church boy personality, though he hadn't been to church since he was fifteen years old and began playing sports. Church activities took up too much of his time, so his grandmother reluctantly approved. She didn't have a choice anyway because he was always going to put more focus on his love of football, and she wasn't about to interfere with his dream.

"Great. I will call my parents tonight to let them know."

Billy thought he was dreaming when he heard his sister's voice outside of his dorm.

"Billy, open this door," she kept repeating. He got up to wipe the drool from his mouth, opened the door, and there stood his sister and Olivia.

"Surprise." Brandy said as she reached to hug her brother.

"What are you doing here and why didn't you tell me you were coming?"

"Do I need permission to see my big-headed brother?"

"No, but I would have liked to know so I could be prepared. How are you, sis? Oh, and hi Olivia." Brandy said everything was fine but she needed to see him. Home wasn't the same without him around and she wanted to see him physically to know that UT in Austin was treating him well. Brandy looked around and asked where Wilt was, but Billy didn't know. He hadn't seen him since last night.

Olivia began surveying Wilt's area and found it neat, which wasn't a surprise because he was a neat freak. She opened his top drawer slightly. Billy asked what she was doing and instructed her to leave his man's things alone. He didn't want to be responsible for her messing up his stuff. Wilt knew where he put everything, and if anything was out of place, Billy didn't want to be accused of snooping or stealing. Olivia obliged, sighed, and sat down in a chair next to his bed.

"So, how is Mama and does she know you are here?"

"You know she would beat the black off me if she knew I was here without her permission."

"Yeah, you're right, and she would have a whole lot of beating to do."

"Forget you, punk." Brandy threw a pillow that barely missed Billy's head.

She told him to get dressed so he could show them the campus because they didn't come to see him in his room all day. While Billy got dressed, there was laughter coming from outside the door. It sounded like Wilt, but the female voice wasn't recognizable. Wilt opened the door and there sat Brandy and Olivia staring at Wilt and Brooke. Olivia couldn't believe it. She wanted to know who the hell this girl was, so without hesitation she moved within inches of Brooke's face and asked.

"Who are you?"

"I'm Brooke."

"And? Like I said, who are you?"

"I'm sorry, I don't understand. I just answered your question. I'm Brooke." She then extended her hand to Olivia to shake but Olivia looked at it like it smelled like dog crap. Her attitude was at an all-time high altitude. So, Wilt intervened and introduced them to each other. He introduced both Brooke and Olivia as his friends.

Billy came out of the bathroom with a toothbrush hanging out of his mouth and toothpaste on his bottom lip, but when he saw all the looks to kill, he decided to go back into the restroom and let Wilt handle his *own* mess.

"Excuse me, I'm Brandy, Billy's sister," Brandy said, greeting Brooke. She rolled her eyes at Wilt because she knew he had secretly been seeing her friend, but now he was trying to act *brand new.* However, the situation wasn't even what Olivia was making it out to be. He took her on a few dates and treated her with respect, but that was it. They were never intimate or anything. Wilt didn't understand Brandy or Olivia's attitudes. Olivia wasn't *his* girl.

Olivia asked to speak with Wilt in private, so they went out in the hallway while Billy was in the bathroom and Brooke and Brandy in the dorm. Olivia asked Wilt again who Brooke was to *him.* She knew her name, but she wanted to know her status and what the hell she was doing with *her* man?

"Olivia, I'm not your man. Going on a few dates doesn't make us exclusive."

"So, I came all the way to Austin for nothing, huh? Our last conversation you said you missed me. What the hell was that supposed to mean?" She began to tear up.

"Olivia, it was true, but things have changed since we spoke a few weeks ago. I'm in college now and you are in high school. I can't be seen with you anymore. I don't want to get into trouble. I'm eighteen and you're barely sixteen."

"Trouble? Well, you should have thought about that a long time ago." She slapped Wilt across his face and said she never wanted to see him again, and told him to lose her number. She stormed back into the room crying, telling Brandy that she was ready to go home. Billy came out of the bathroom, saw Olivia crying, and immediately got on Wilt.

"What's going on? What did you do to her?"

"Man, I didn't do anything, she was the one that just slapped me." "Well, you probably deserved it. Your player card needs to be revoked." Billy took Olivia in his arms and tried to comfort her like a little sister, but she kept crying while Brooke stood there confused. Brooke said it was time for her to leave and told Wilt to call her. He agreed and walked her out the door while apologizing profusely. He said he would explain it all to her later. He hugged and kissed her on the cheek and walked her out of the residence hall.

Chapter Fourteen

Sasha drove Barbara home so that she could get a change of clothes for their "girls' day out." Barbara quickly showered, put on a pair of jeans, and a silk gold blouse along with her two-inch heel-fringe boots. She came downstairs looking for Sasha but couldn't find her. She went into her room and saw Sasha holding the football that Billy had given her. Sasha wanted to bring up the *friendship* between Barbara and Billy but didn't know when would be the appropriate time. Her cousin was going through so many things that were massive compared to her rocky relationship with Billy.

"You know, if you want, you can have the football," Barbara said when she saw Sasha in her room holding it tightly.

"No, he gave it to you because he wanted *you* to have it." Sasha placed the football back in its original place and complimented Barbara on how nice she looked. Her hips and butt had filled out into a nice hourglass shape. She had to give it to her cousin, her body was one to die for.

"So, are you ready to go to my house so your mom can meet us there?"

"No, I texted her earlier letting her know I was going home to change clothes and she could pick us up there instead of traveling back to your house."

Barbara said her mom mentioned she was meeting Aunt Lizzy, so she might be a little late depending on how their meeting went, and traffic. Sasha began talking about their mothers' relationship and how she couldn't imagine not being close to her sister if she had one. They pondered what might have happened to strain the relationship, and were happy to be meeting Jenny so she could tell them everything. It was something that they loved about Jenny. She didn't know what tact was and didn't mince words.

"Do you want to go to the hospital and see how my dad is doing? We will be back in time to meet my mom."

Barbara didn't have to ask Sasha twice; they were at Methodist Hospital within fifteen minutes. And as soon as she opened the door to her father's room he sat up in bed and his eyes lit up like he hadn't seen her in ages.

"Hey, there's my girl." Barbara dashed into his arms like a child and he held her tight. "Hi Uncle, how you?" Sasha asked as she came to embrace him. He said that he might be released that day or the next, depending on his vitals. He wanted to know what time Barbara's flight left for Washington because he needed someone to pick him up. Sasha volunteered but he said that he would get his sister if Barbara wasn't available.

"Where are you two going looking all nice and smelling good?"

"We are going to meet my mother for a girls' day out."

Leon looked concerned. He didn't want Barbara around her mother without him being there. He didn't want her poisoning his daughter with lies and wished that she hadn't come into town. He still loved Jenny with all his heart, but he knew that her secrets would tear his life apart. He didn't know what to do to stop her and make her go back to where she came from. Barbara noticed the change in his demeanor when she mentioned her mother. She knew that her father was hiding something. She didn't know what, but she would find out eventually. She looked down at her phone and saw a text from Jenny saying that she was running a little late but would be there soon. Barbara and Sasha visited thirty minutes longer with Leon before they left to meet Jenny.

They arrived home and saw Kurt driving by her house. He noticed Barbara in the car with Sasha and immediately turned around. He killed the car engine and could hardly wait for her to exit the car. When she got out, he grabbed her and spun her around. He asked when she'd gotten back to town and said how he'd missed her. He greeted Sasha, but it was Barbara he was happy to see, and she was happy to see him too. They talked about his new job and how he elected to go to a trade school instead of college. He wanted to be an entrepreneur and was working on opening his own plumbing business. Barbara asked if he wanted to come inside, but he declined. He had errands to run but offered to come by later if it was okay with her. She said it was fine, and she would see him soon. She watched him drive off before opening the front door to wait for her mother to arrive.

It had been over an hour since her mother texted and said she was on her way, but she hadn't arrived. Barbara called her cell phone but it went straight to her voicemail. She called the hotel room and spoke to Hakeem, but he hadn't seen her since that morning when she left to meet Lizzy. Sasha called her mother, who said Jenny left her over an hour ago and that she could be stuck in traffic.

Three hours later, Jenny still hadn't arrived or answered her phone, and Barbara was beginning to worry. She knew her mother had left in the middle of the night without a word when she was eight years old, but this felt different. Sasha called her mother again to let her know that Jenny still hadn't arrived, but Lizzy assured her that she was just being Jenny and she had been fine when she left their meeting.

Leon called Barbara to see how her day was going with her mother. She told him that she never arrived and that they were at his house still waiting for her.

"Oh God, she probably did it again," he said.

"Did what again?" Barbara asked.

"Ran away. That's what she has done all her life was run away instead of face adversity head on. Her remedy has always been to run."

"But Dad, she just got home, and she wanted to be in my life. It doesn't make any sense."

Barbara was worried about Jenny but Leon said not to worry and to just accept it as something she did. It was one of the reasons he wished she hadn't returned. His daughter had been doing fine without her and now she had returned only to reenact her disappearing act like she did ten years ago. Barbara reluctantly agreed with her dad and couldn't help but feel abandoned all over again.

"Do you want to get something to eat and then go to my house for the night?" Sasha asked.

"No, I'm fine. I will wait here in case she shows up." Sasha told Barbara to call her if she changed her mind and Barbara agreed that she would. After seeing Sasha off, she went into her bedroom and let out a loud scream.

"Why, Mommy, why?" She fell to her knees and cried, folding her knees and wrapping her arms around them in a fetal position. She longed for her mother and wished it was reciprocated.

Suzie walked past the nurse's station and straight to her brother's room. A hanger she carried had a pair of freshly-ironed blue jeans, a white polo shirt, and in her other hand she held a pair of Leon's favorite sneakers. It was finally time for him to be released from the hospital. She tapped lightly on the door because she heard voices inside. Barbara was embracing her father before she caught her flight back to Howard. She turned to hug her aunt and then she was out the door because she only had an hour to check in at the airport. She decided to take a cab and not wake Sasha since she had spent all night crying on the phone about her mother's whereabouts. Her brown eyes were red and puffy. Suzie wanted to know what was wrong, but Barbara quickly said it was nothing and she had to hurry because her cab was waiting for her downstairs. Suzie asked why she hadn't called her to take her to the airport but Barbara looked away and turned to leave. She was too emotional to answer. Besides, she didn't want to hear a lecture about her mother. Suzie looked at her brother.

"What is wrong with her?"

Leon sighed and said, "You really don't want to know."

"Why do you think I asked if I didn't want to know?"

Leon didn't know where to start so he began talking about Jenny and her disappearing acts. How she never came to pick Barbara and Sasha up for their girls' day out and hadn't called. Barbara felt abandoned all over again like when Jenny left ten years ago.

"I don't know why Jenny does the things she does. I swear she needs to get her head examined. Poor Barbara don't need to be wrapped up in all this mess."

"I know. I know. Sometimes I just wish she'd go and stay. Out of sight, out of mind." He expressed to his sister that he was worried about Barbara and asked her to take a leave of absence from school, but she wouldn't think of it. She wanted to finish her education and return home to teach.

"You know how strong headed Barbara is. She gets it from her mother."

"Yeah, I'm trying to figure out if that's a good or bad thing," Suzie said, rolling her eyes up to the ceiling. She asked if Leon had been discharged and he said that he was waiting for the official doctor's orders, but as soon as he said it the nurse walked in and had him sign the discharge papers. He was free to leave. The nurse said that she would send the orderly in with a wheelchair to assist him to the car. Leon took the clothes from his sister to get dressed while she went downstairs to get the car ready.

Ten minutes later the male orderly helped Leon into the chair and they headed to the front entrance where Suzie was parked. She got out of the car to open the door and the orderly helped Leon into the passenger's seat.

"You take care of yourself, Mr. Knight," the orderly said as he folded the wheelchair.

"Thank you, sir, and I appreciate everything." Leon reached out to give him a final handshake.

Suzie thanked the orderly, got into the car, and they were headed home. She asked if Leon wanted to stay with her for a few days, but he refused. He was more than ready to get back to his life and felt that he needed to do it by himself. He didn't want to be treated like a charity or sympathy case. He was a man that took care of his family and responsibilities.

"When are you going to tell Barbara what Jenny came to tell her?" Suzie asked, catching Leon off guard because he was not ready to hear this conversation and never would be.

"Suzie, I just got home. I don't want to talk about it right now."

"Well, you can't keep avoiding it. I mean, the truth is bound to come out anyway. She may as well hear it from you."

Leon knew his sister was right. She was always right and had given him motherly advice ever since their biological mother unexpectedly passed away when Leon was fifteen. She was the older sister who took him under her wing and made sure he finished high school and college. She even told him to go into a career field of math, science, or engineering. He respected her because she was all that he had growing up.

"You want to stop and get something to eat? You have groceries?" "Barbara said she went to the store and bought some things and cooked a casserole for me. She knew I was coming home today, so she took care of everything."

"You're lucky to have her and that's the reason she needs to hear the *truth* from you. Now, you think about what I told you before you lose her. You done already lost Jenny." Leon stopped her before she went on a long righteous tirade. He said that he would before he exited the car.

"You sure you don't need me to walk you inside?" Leon didn't say a word. He closed the car door and gestured to her by walking and throwing his hand up without even turning around. He spoke to Mrs. Wilson, and she told him she was glad to see him and welcome back home. She offered her help as well, but Leon didn't need it. He just needed some rest and some alone time.

Chapter Fifteen

It has been four years and still no word from my mother, Barbara thought as she looked out the dormitory window. She called many times only to get her voicemail, and after a year of unanswered calls, she decided it was time to move on and focus on school.

She completed college and the commencement ceremonies were two weeks away. Phillip, her boyfriend, was helping her pack her things to move back home. It was almost Christmas, and the weather was frigid as snow flurries fell diagonally to the pavement and onto the dormant St. Augustine grass. She couldn't wait to get back home to Texas and a warmer climate. She checked the weather in San Antonio and temperatures were in the sixties.

She stood looking out at the students dressed in winter attire. Many had packed their bags and were set to leave Howard as well. She wore her Eddie Bauer trench coat, scarf, and leather gloves as she held her Bison mascot mug and sipped on her hot chocolate. She reflected on when she first met Phillip, finding the very spot underneath a maple tree where he approached her. He was tall, brown skinned, and handsome was an understatement. He had the whitest teeth and the sincerest smile. He was all that she could ask for in a boyfriend. He was a listener, not much of a talker, but he analyzed and paid attention to everything she ever said or didn't say. He was a mind reader. He had a special gift of knowing what she thought before she said anything. It was a gift and a curse because she could never say "nothing" when he asked if something was bothering her.

He was going to school to become an attorney and someday a judge. He was not only intelligent, but he was patient. He respected Barbara and her wish to save her virginity until *after* marriage, and he agreed that loyalty and family meant everything. Family meaning a two-parent household with both parents involved in raising the children. She didn't want a repeat of what her mother had done to her. She would never abandon her children. She would raise them with love and compassion.

Phillip entered the dorm room after packing her last set of items.

"You ready to go, Barb?"

"Yes, Phil. I'm ready as ever." They shortened each other's first names, not intentionally, but out of habit. It was an act of endearment.

Leaving Howard was bittersweet. She was going to miss the place that helped her escape the reality of what was happening back home. It was a place of Black culture, pride, unity, and solace. She learned so much about Black Americans and Africa by attending an Historically Black College and University, and graduating with zero student loan debt was like a hammer to the nail. It was a done sealed deal.

Barbara first visited her friend Amy, telling her to stay in touch and that she'd see her at the graduation ceremony. She saved the best for last by saying bye to Cathy, also known as Coco. Coco was a character. She had another year left because she had to take a few semesters off due to pregnancy. Unfortunately, she lost her baby boy to SIDS. Barbara cried and held Coco tight and didn't want to let go. Coco being the "strong" Black woman told her to get on out of there before she made her cry.

"Phillip, come get your girl," Coco demanded as she wiped the corner of her eye, trying not to let anyone see her tears.

"You better stay in touch. Don't let me have to come down to Texas," she said.

Barbara shook her head and promised she would. Phillip placed his hand on Barbara's back and told her it was time to go. She did as she was told and walked out of Howard University for the last time. She looked back at the campus and all the wonderful memories, then placed her hand against her heart and murmured, "Thank you."

Phillip opened the car door and she reluctantly got inside. He slowly pulled away to let her inhale and exhale as she looked through the thick laminated glass to the snow flurries outside the window.

Phillip was going back to his hometown in Houston and would be driving to San Antonio the following week. When they arrived at the airport they embraced for what felt like hours, and then Phil watched as his Barb walked up the jetway to board her flight. His plane would leave an hour after hers. She waved and blew him a kiss, which he caught and placed in his pocket for safe keepings. His smile was all she needed to have a safe flight.

Leon arrived at the airport early. He couldn't wait to see his daughter. It had been a while since she visited after his release from the hospital, and every time they talked, he avoided all the unanswered questions about her mother. She stayed away because she wanted him to know that she was no longer a *little* girl but a young woman, and all the secrets that he held had affected her mentally. He tried to protect her, but he couldn't understand how much the abandonment hurt.

She saw him first, ran behind him, and covered his eyes.

"Is that my Pumpkin?" He turned around and hardly recognized her. Her natural hair had grown to a big coily afro, and she wore a rose hair clip on the left side. She had exchanged her glasses for contact lenses.

"Let me look at you." He said as Barbara turned around and walked the runway like a model. She gushed and held her arms out for a hug. She looked around for Sasha since she was supposed to be with her father.

"Billy came home yesterday. She called and said that she wasn't going to be able to make it, but made plans for you two to go out after you arrived."

"Plans? She never told me about any plans to go out."

"I'm sure she didn't. You know how Sasha is."

Barbara laughed because she knew her cousin all too well.

It was warm in the airport, and she felt kind of silly in winter clothing when it was sixty-six degrees in San Antonio. She took off her coat, scarf, and gloves and put them across the luggage that her father held tight. Leon asked if she was hungry and wanted to get something to eat before heading home. She wanted her vegetarian pizza, but no less than ten minutes after heading to Pizza Hut, Barbara was fast asleep. The emotional good-byes and jetlag had gotten the best of her. Leon ordered the food before leaving the airport so when they arrived, their order was ready. He paid and tipped the cashier, and they were on their way home.

The car stopped and Barbara didn't recognize her own neighborhood. A Walmart had been built right up the street and there was more traffic than usual. The neighborhood was filled with Christmas decor and so was her house. She got out of the car and walked straight to her room. She saw the eight-foot Christmas tree when she entered the house but was too tired to relish how beautiful it was. She took off her shoes and lay down in bed. Leon unloaded her luggage, took everything to her room, and saw that she had passed out. He decided not to wake her so she could eat because he knew she was drained. He took her cell phone out of her hand and silenced it so she wouldn't be disturbed. When he silenced her phone, he saw three missed calls and a text from an unknown number.

"Barbara, this is your mother. Please call me at this number. I have so much I want to tell you."

Leon's hands shook with anxiety and anger as he read the text message. He didn't know whether to call Jenny or delete the message. He picked up the cell phone and began to dial, **555-384-710** but his nervousness wouldn't allow him to press the last digit. He wanted Jenny to disappear and hated that she kept playing mind games with Barbara. So instead of calling her, he hit the delete button. When it asked, **are you sure you want to delete the message,** he pressed **yes**. Barbara stirred and saw her father holding her phone. She asked if everything was okay. He placed the phone on the bedside table and told her that everything was fine and to rest easy. He closed her bedroom door and went into his bedroom to call Lizzy.

Billy walked into the kitchen to grab himself a bite to eat. He and Wilt arrived at home the day before. He was with Sasha the entire day and night, and she'd just left to go home and get a change of clothes. She was excited because she knew Barbara would be home today and she'd made plans to go out. Billy hadn't seen his friend for years because she hadn't been home, even for the holidays. He texted and called her a few times just to check on her, and she would always say everything was good. He told her to call if she ever needed anything. She never did, but he called her once because he needed assistance in his finance course. Who would have ever thought he would graduate with a bachelor's in finance? His promise to his mother was his word and he was true to it.

Brandy and her best friend Olivia were in their sophomore year at Rice University. She was coming home this weekend. He hadn't seen her since last Christmas.

Billy knocked on his mother's door to ask what she was doing, and she welcomed him in for a talk.

"You know I'm so proud of you. You are all that I knew you would be."

"I'm not finished though, Mama. I'm just getting started. I'm expected to be in the top ten of the NFL draft next year. Have you started looking at where you wanted to move to?"

"Billy, you know I'm fine right where I am. This was my first home with your father, where we raised you and your sister. I'm not trying to leave my memories."

"Aw…Mama, it's time to make new memories and start dating again. You're too young and gorgeous and *you look just like me*. Besides, I know Pops would want you to move on."

Melody loved her son and thought he was something else. He always spoke what was on his mind.

"Humph, *I* look just like *you*, huh?" No, you look just like me." She corrected him, but he said it didn't matter who looked like who. The point was that she was *beautiful* and needed to go out and find herself a *man*.

"Mama, can I ask you a question?"

"Naw, Billy, cause ain't no telling what you're going to say."

"Naw, Mama. I'm serious, can I?"

"Billy, what did I say?"

He ignored her and asked anyway,

"When was the last time you got your groove on?" His mother laughed, flapping her feet, and shouted "boy" with embarrassment. She threw her pillow at him and told him to get on out of her bedroom. Billy laughed, got up off the bed, and told her, "You know Stella got her groove back. It ain't too late fo' you, Mama." His mother laughed until her heart almost stopped. He tickled her pink as he kept singing through her bedroom door, "Ged yo groove back, Mama. Ged it back, Ged it back."

Billy heard the front door open and a whiney voice called, "What y'all in here laughing about? Where Mama at?"

Brandy opened her mother's bedroom door and saw her laughing and covering her mouth. She saw Brandy and immediately jumped up to hug her baby. She wasn't expecting her to be home until later that week. She said that she and Olivia decided to leave after finals instead of waiting.

"Mama, what Billy in here telling you that got you blushing?" Billy began dancing and gyrating his hips singing, "I told yo' Mama to ged her groove back, ged it back, ged it back."

"Ooohhh, you nasty, don't be telling *my* mama to be no hootchie."

"I ain't told her to be no hootchie, I said, 'Ged yo' groove back. Ged yo' groove back. Ged it, ged it back.'" He continued to sing and dance while gyrating his hips. Brandy and Melody couldn't help but laugh. He was another Chris Tucker in disguise. He was the life of the Daye family and Melody was elated to have both of her kids home for Christmas.

Chapter Sixteen

The graduation ceremonies were officially over and Sasha and Barbara, the college graduates, were in the mood for some last-minute Christmas shopping. Phillip was down from Houston, and he was spending time with Leon. Barbara was reluctant to leave him alone with her dad because she didn't know what to expect. She called every hour to check in on him, but she heard yelling in the background and a basketball game on TV, so she knew both men were good.

Christmas dinner would be hosted at Leon's home this year instead of being held at Lizzy's house. Barbara and Sasha had decided they would cook dinner for the family. Lizzy and Suzie were reluctant and offered their assistance, which was appreciated but not needed. It was time for them to pass the torch to Barbara and Sasha and let them cater to them.

Sasha had met Phillip the other night and thought he was *fine.* She wanted to know what Barbara was getting him for Christmas. Barbara was considering a nice watch or a tie.

"A tie? How long have you been dating?"

"It's been about a year. Why?"

"I'm just asking. I was thinking the brother needs more than a tie."

Barbara explained how easy to please Phil was and how his lack of materialism was what she admired most about him.

"I wonder what he's getting you?"

"I don't know. It's the thought that counts."

"Umm, that's all fine and dandy and the politically correct answer. But Billy better get me something special."

"And what if he doesn't?"

"Girl, he *better.* I don't even want to think about how I will react if he doesn't." Sasha was being petty. She knew Billy was a good man and Christmas was supposed to be least about receiving and more about giving.

"Oh, by the way, do you have any gently-worn clothes that you no longer wear?" Barbara asked. "I'm collecting some items to donate to the San Antonio Women and Children's shelters."

"I do have some clothes that are too small. I've gained so much weight." Sasha turned to look at her butt through the store window.

"Sasha. Seriously? Ten pounds if that?"

"It doesn't matter. I got to stay in shape because Billy is going to the NFL, and you know how groupies are."

Barbara laughed about Sasha's insecurities and said groupies and other women didn't matter because a loyal man would always be a good man. It was another politically-correct answer that Sasha wasn't trying to hear. She wanted to keep herself looking good for her *loyal man*. She was going to look the best she could to keep him.

"Anyway, yeah. I will get the clothes together for you tomorrow."

Two hours later, with shopping bags stuffed everywhere in the back of the Toyota Corolla Barbara got for her eighteenth birthday, it was time to retire home for the day. They were going to open mic night with Brandy and Olivia, who were at the shop getting their hair and nails done. It was going to be ladies' night and they couldn't wait.

Barbara pulled into the driveway after taking Sasha to Billy's house to get dressed. She struggled with her bags but didn't want any help so her father and Phil wouldn't see what she bought them.

"Barbara Knight? Is that you?" A familiar voice called out as soon as she closed the trunk of her car. She couldn't believe it; it was Kurt. He had cut his hair and was dressed in a black Armani business suit with a gold and black tie. He looked totally different from the last time she'd seen him.

"Let me help you with those bags," he insisted without giving her a chance to object.

He grabbed them *all* from her hand. She smiled and inhaled his Dolce & Gabbana cologne. He looked so good. He said he was on his way to his little cousin's graduation ceremony and happened to see her drive up. He wanted to know how long she would be in town, and she said she was home to stay. He was elated to hear this and mentioned that he'd opened his own plumbing company and gave her one of his business cards. She invited him for Christmas dinner if he didn't have any plans. He didn't, so he accepted. They talked for about ten minutes before she took the bags from him and went inside.

"Hey Barb, let me help you with those bags?" Phillip offered as he saw Barbara coming through the door.

"No, I got them. I don't want you or my dad to see what's inside." She took the bags to her room and placed them in her closet. As soon as she closed the closet door, Phillip was on her heels asking how her shopping trip was. He really wanted to ask who Kurt was but decided it didn't seem like a big deal. Still, he was taking notice. He also asked about the football in her room that Billy had given her. She explained to him that it was from her cousin's boyfriend who she helped tutor in math. She changed the subject and wanted to know about his day with her father.

"Are you enjoying yourself with my dad?"

Phillip drew Barbara near and placed his hand at her waist. He looked into her eyes and told her how lucky he was, and that her dad was amazing. They were getting ready to grill steaks on the barbecue pit.

"I'm glad my father is being a good host. My cousin and some friends and I are going to an open mic event. Is that okay with you?" He said it was all good because he and Leon were going to barbecue and watch the game.

"I really appreciate you spending time with my dad. He doesn't have many friends, and ever since his accident, he hasn't really been the same." In all honesty, Barbara still had the police report stating that her father had tried to kill himself fresh on her mind. She hadn't asked him about it and was waiting for him to explain why and how the incident occurred. But trying to get information from her father was like pulling teeth.

"Are you two going to be up here all day or are you coming to join me?" Leon interrupted, letting Phillip know that the game was on, and he was about to fire up the barbecue pit. He told Barbara he had vegetable shish kabobs and grilled potatoes for her, and for them to come join him.

Barbara told Phillip to go ahead. She was going to wash up and then join them. Leon asked Phillip to put the steaks on the grill because he wanted to talk with Barbara. Phillip left and Leon sat on Barbara's bed while she was washing up and checking her hair and makeup. Barbara's phone beeped and Leon didn't know whether to read the text message or not. It beeped again and he reluctantly picked up her phone and saw another message from Jenny.

"Barbara, please call me back at this number."
"It's important."

Leon immediately deleted the messages and placed the phone where it was before beginning his conversation with Barbara.

"So, you really like Phillip, huh?"

Barbara came out of the bathroom and placed her hands on her hips as if to say she couldn't believe her dad was asking her that question like she was in high school. She didn't say anything, but played along and said she *really* liked him, and Phillip was a good guy who reminded her of Leon. Leon was taken aback by the compliment, but felt kind of guilty, especially since he had been deleting her text messages from her mother. He didn't want Phillip to be anything like him because a guy like him wasn't good enough for his daughter.

"Have you vetted him?" she asked. "But most importantly, did he pass the test?"

Leon stood and placed his arms around her. "With flying colors."

They both laughed and decided to join Phillip outside on the back patio.

Two hours later, after great conversation, laughs, and full stomachs, Barbara excused herself because she needed to take a shower and get dressed for the night's events. She phoned Sasha and Brandy, and they were still on for the evening and couldn't wait. Brandy contacted Olivia and they decided to meet at her house since Sasha was there with Billy.

Leon and Phillip talked about everything from stocks, bonds, Roth IRAs, sports, politics, cars, school, his daughter, and family. Barbara came outside wearing a burgundy silk dress with a floral head wrap to accentuate her complexion, she wore burgundy stilettos and ankh earrings that matched her head wrap. Her Mac makeup and lip gloss were flawless. She looked and smelled amazing and was ready to turn heads and stop traffic.

"Look at you. Phillip, you are the luckiest man in the world."

Phillip corrected Leon, saying that he was the *happiest* man in the world as he reached for Barbara to give her a soft kiss on her cheek. Barbara gleamed with confidence and pride. She had two men who adored her, what more could she ask for? Barbara's phone rang and Leon jumped and clutched his chest praying that it wasn't Jenny. She answered after the third ring.

"Hey, yes, I'm on my way." Leon breathed a sigh of relief that it wasn't Jenny. Barbara noticed Leon's expression and wondered why he was so nervous when her phone rang. She took a mental note like she has been doing for the past four years.

"That was Sasha. She wants to get good seats, so I must be going. Dad, you know how she is." Leon shook his head because he knew how impatient his niece was. Barbara kissed her dad goodnight and Phillip walked her to the car, but he couldn't keep his hands off her. He hugged and kissed her tightly and didn't want to let her go.

"Phil, Sasha is going to kill me if I don't get there on time. I have to go," she said as she pulled his hands away from her waist.

"I love you, Barb," were Phil's last words before he watched her get into the car and drive out of sight.

Billy and Wilt were outside playing a game of two-on-two basketball when Barbara pulled up. She got out of the car and started walking toward them. Billy couldn't believe his eyes and had to do a double take. He thought to himself, *Damn.*

"Damn girl, can I get with you?" Wilt said, voicing Billy's thoughts out loud. He was intoxicated, not only by her beauty, but the sweet smell of her perfume. Billy, drenched in sweat and smelling like musty cologne, greeted her with a fist bump even though a hug would have been better.

"Hey guys. I see y'all getting a workout in and having fun at the same time." Barbara said as she pinched Billy's love handles. He swatted her hand away in jest, telling her that his BMI was at the *optimal* level. She said, "According to which BMI chart?"

"I see you *still* got jokes, huh?" Billy laughed and Wilt agreed with Barbara. She kept joking about his weight, so Billy surprisingly grabbed her, sweat dripping down his shirtless Greek God body. He picked her up, spun her around, and asked if BMI could do that? Before putting her down, he gave her a kiss on the forehead. It not only shocked her, but Sasha as well, who saw the entire interaction between Billy and Barbara.

"Ugh. Billy, put me down with yo' sweaty self." She swiped downward, fixing and adjusting her dress to make sure it didn't get wrinkled. But she couldn't help wondering what the kiss was for. She decided to ignore it when she saw Sasha coming out of the front door, Brandy and Olivia fast on her heels.

"Bout time. I hope we don't miss the start of the show," Sasha hissed.

Barbara tried to explain that Phillip was in town, and they'd had a barbecue and she'd needed to see him off before she left. Sasha didn't care. She'd seen *her man picking her up and kissing her* and that's all she could focus on. She wanted to know if there was something *more* than friendship between them. She began walking to Barbara's car, not saying a word to Billy, and sat on the passenger side. Brandy looked at her brother and shook her head, following Sasha to the car. Olivia, giddy over seeing Wilt, told him "Bye." He waved her off like an annoying gnat. Billy looked at Barbara and shrugged his shoulders like, "*What did I do wrong*?" He was oblivious to how everyone else perceived them. Their chemistry couldn't be hidden. A blind man could see that it was something more than friendship. Barbara got into the car, but before she could drive off, Billy called out and jogged to the car to kiss Sasha. She rolled up her window and pulled down her sun visor to check her appearance, completely ignoring him. She signaled for Barbara to go, and she did as she was told.

"Ah ha. She dissed yo' ass."

Billy threw the ball at Wilt and told him to worry about Brooke and how she would feel about him talking to Olivia.

"This ain't about me and you know it. You need to stop playing mind games with yo' girl because you know you got it bad for Barbara.

"Man, play ball. Ain't nobody got it bad for Barbara. She's just my friend." Wilt told him to stop lying to himself and admit he was in *love* with the other cousin.

Barbara, Sasha, Brandy, and Olivia arrived at the open mic club just in time to get great seats. When they walked in, Destiny Child's "Jumpin', Jumpin'" blasted through the speakers. Strobe lights lit up the Black art lining the walls, along with framed photographs of some of the greatest artists. Smokey Robinson, Marvin Gaye, Tammi Terrell, and poets James Baldwin, Maya Angelo, and Toni Morrison. A handsome deejay swayed to the music, scratching the vinyl record with headphones covering his ears. He stood five feet ten inches tall, a chiseled statue with dreadlocks and a light honey complexion. Two men stood next to him rocking to the music and giving each other dap.

"I'm thirsty and going to get a drink. Does anybody want anything?" Sasha asked, speaking louder than normal because of the music. Barbara, Brandy, and Olivia wanted a Sprite.

When Sasha walked to the bar to get drinks, the deejay's eyes followed her baby blue dress. It had a slit going up to the middle of her thighs, and her shoes and pursed matched. She sat on a stool waiting for the bartender to take her order. A deep masculine voice came up from behind her and startled her.

"How are you doing, lovely lady? But most importantly, can I buy you a drink?"

Sasha turned and there stood the sexy-ass deejay. She crossed her legs and responded. "Only if you would buy my friends one too." She pointed at her girls sitting at the table waiting for their Sprite sodas. The deejay immediately called the bartender, even though he was in the middle of another order, and advised him to get whatever the lady wanted and to put it on his tab. He then slid Sasha his business card and told her he had to get back to work, but maybe he could have a dance and her number before she left. She looked down at his card.

DJ Mr. Rashad Lewis
210-555-1411
Mixing Hip hop, Blues, R&B music

It had a picture of Rashad with a record player, mixing and scratching a record. Sasha thought, *impressive and cute*. Except she wasn't referring to the card but rather the deejay who handed it to her. She opened her purse and placed it inside.

"I think I can make that happen. Do you have a pen?"

Rashad asked the bartender for a pen and a piece of paper. Sasha was happy that he asked the bartender because it would have been a red flag if had he pulled them out himself. It would have let her know that getting numbers was his *regular* routine. She wrote her number down, handed the paper to him, and he quickly placed it in his pocket. He smiled and told her he would see her soon and to *please* save the last dance for him. She responded with a smile and watched his fine ass walk away.

Sasha returned to the table with four Sprites. Her attitude had changed in a matter of minutes upon arrival. The car ride had been library silent. Even Brandy and Olivia weren't chattering like they normally did. The radio could hardly be heard because everyone was deep in their thoughts. Barbara questioned, *why did Billy kiss me?* Sasha had the same thought as Barbara and wondered, *Does Billy like my cousin?* Brandy thought about her brother playing both of her friends, whom she admired. But Olivia's thoughts were on Wilt's shirtless body parts.

Barbara, Brandy, and Olivia thanked Sasha for the drinks. Sasha let it be known not to thank her but the deejay as she waved at him. He winked and smiled at her as she placed her straw into her Sprite and sipped it. Rashad and Sasha couldn't keep their eyes off each other the entire night. Barbara noticed and nudged her, whispering in her ear, "I see you and the deejay made a connection. I would tread lightly because *Brandy is Billy's sister.*"

Sasha couldn't have cared less. She was upset at her man and the way to forget about him kissing her cousin was to take it out on another man. Rashad wasn't any man, though. He was sexy and his cologne danced through her nostrils. She was really feeling him but was uncertain if the Billy incident was making Rashad even more attractive. Was anger driving her toward him?

Open mic ended and the deejay slowed it down with some R&B smooth jams. The dance floor was packed with patrons. Brandy and Olivia were in the ladies' room when Rashad walked to the table and introduced himself to Barbara. He then asked Sasha for a dance. She couldn't jump out of her seat fast enough. She stood to readjust her dress as Rashad held out his hand and guided her to the dance floor.

Tony Terry's "With You" stole the show as Sasha and Rashad entered their own world. He held her close, and she felt secure. Something she had never felt before, even with Billy. Her head rested upon his chest, and his right hand found a comfortable place around her lower back; their opposite hands held tight as their bodies two-stepped to the beautiful melody and lyrics. The song ended and another one started playing that jarred Sasha to reality. She asked if Rashad needed to get back to work, and he whispered in her ear, "Naw, I got this, just relax."

After three songs, Barbara wondered if her cousin was going to come back to earth because the look on Brandy's face watching her hugged up with Rashad didn't sit well. She even saw her take a picture of Sasha and Rashad and hoped she didn't text it to her brother. Barbara tried striking up a conversation with Brandy to get her mind off what she was seeing but it was useless. She kept watching and taking pictures until she was asked to dance, but she declined. Instead, Olivia happily accepted. By the time Olivia got on the dance floor the slow jams had ended and hip hop was in full effect. Sasha returned to the table as the deejay took his rightful place back into the booth.

"Looked like you were *single* and having a good time," Brandy hissed. Sasha smiled and said, "I am and I was. I don't see a ring on my finger." She looked down at her left-hand ring finger and it was bare.

Brandy rolled her eyes and thought to herself: *Let's see what my brother thinks about this. Yeah, you gon' be single all right.*

Melody opened the front door to her home and saw her son asleep on the couch while a UT football video played. He immediately woke up when he heard her trying to creep past him. He noticed her dressed in regular clothes and not her work uniform.

"Nun uh, Mama where you been?"

She clenched her chest and shouted. "Billy, you scared the heck out of me. I thought you were asleep."

"Naw, I ain't asleep. I've been up watching video and wondering where *you've* been."

She asked him why he was home alone and asked where Sasha was. He told her she was out with Brandy, and not to try and change the subject. He wanted to know where she'd been. She told him that it was none of his business.

"You're my mama. Of course, it's *my* business."

Melody was flattered but she didn't want her son to feel that she was his responsibility, or that since his father's death he must be the man of the house. It wasn't right and she didn't want to put him in that role or under that kind of pressure. She decided to give him an explanation because he wasn't going to let it go.

"Ole Billy, if you *must* know. I was on date."

Billy sat up and said, "Mama, what?"

She told him that she took what he'd told her into consideration, but she'd secretly been seeing someone for about two months.

"Mama, what you talkin' bout? You've *been* getting your groove on?" He smiled and waited for her to reply.

She laughed and said, "No, it wasn't like that." And before she could go any further he insisted that he wanted to meet the guy.

"Anybody that's going to be getting their freak on with *my* Mama, I got to meet him."

"Billy, I don't know. You and your sister need to act right before I introduce him."

When she said that, Brandy walked in from her eventful time at the club to find her mom and Billy talking. She asked what they were doing, and Billy immediately filled her in.

"Billy, you're the one that told Mama to go be a hootchie. But it looks like she's not the only one." Billy ignored Brandy's comment about his mother not being the *only* hootchie and continued going at his mother.

"I don't care what you talkin' about, Brandy. I need to meet the man that has my mama's nose wide open." Melody and Brandy chuckled because Billy could be so dramatic, puffing out his chest and beating it like he had authority. Brandy said he looked more like *Tarzan, the chimp of the jungle*. Melody said she was going to bed and didn't have time to be foolin' 'round with them. Billy said goodnight as he emphasized, "I still want to meet ole mystery dude." And then he sang and danced around the room, *Mama got her groove back. She got it back.* Melody retired to her room laughing and gasping for air. Her children were the life of her party, the center of her universe. She didn't know where she would be without their love.

Brandy sat down next to Billy after laughing and joking and struck up a serious conversation about his relationship with Sasha. She pulled out her cell phone to show him the pictures of Rashad and Sasha but decided not to, yet. Billy wanted to know why she was all up in his business and declared that he loved Sasha and she was his future wife, even though he felt it was none of Brandy's business. Brandy saw the look in her brother's eyes, realized he really loved her, and placed the cell phone back into her purse. She couldn't steal his joy, especially a few days before Christmas.

"By the way, where is Sasha?" he asked.

"Barbara dropped her off at home first."

Billy didn't say a word. He grabbed his blanket, lay back on the couch and covered himself. He pressed play on the TV remote to finish watching videos. Brandy softly kissed him on the cheek and said that she loved him. She went to her room trying to decide when she was going to tell Billy about his *future wife*.

Chapter Seventeen

Billy called Sasha twice with no response. He left a message and sat awaiting her call back. His mother and sister were both going out to shop and get their hair done for Christmas, which was only two days away. Brandy was helping her mother pick out a nice dress because she couldn't have her mother looking *tore up* when she met her male friend's entire family for the first time. Melody would see how well it went with his family before she introduced him to her children.

Melody, Billy, and Brandy were going to have their traditional holiday gathering with each other and then Melody would meet her *friend* and his family. Brandy and Billy were invited to Barbara's for Christmas dinner.

Billy's phone rang and he picked up immediately.

"Hey Billy, what you doing?" Wilt said.

"Talking to *you* on the phone."

"Man, quit playing. I'm serious. I need to go shopping for Brooke and I wanted to know if you've already got yo girl something?" Wilt was the last person Billy wanted to hear from, but he was the only one who could get his mind off the distance that had opened between him and Sasha since she went to open mic night.

"Man, I have no idea what I'm going to get Sasha. I thought about a few things. But yeah, go ahead and swing by and I'll roll with you."

"Aiight, be there in ten."

As soon as he hung up the phone, he heard a knock at the door, and there stood Wilt. Billy couldn't believe it since he said that he would be there in ten minutes.

"Man, I meant ten seconds, not minutes. You ready to go?"

Billy thought about how silly Wilt was, grabbed his jacket, and went to check his appearance before they left. They decided to take Billy's car because Wilt's *putt-putt,* as he called his car, had no AC or heater, and the sound system was enough to drive a deaf person crazy. They got in Billy's car and Wilt turned up the music real loud. Usually, Billy would check him to turn it down, but not today. He needed anything to drown out his thoughts about Sasha.

"This my jam right here." Wilt said as he began to do the cabbage patch dance to Doug E. Fresh's "The Show." Wilt cuffed his hands to his mouth and began beatboxing, except there was more spit hitting the dashboard than sounds. Billy died laughing because he had watched Wilt trying to master it for years.

"Just give it up, son," Billy teased but Wilt was relentless about learning to beatbox and called him a hater.

"A hater of what? Saliva and germs all over my car's dashboard? When you start making money, you're getting my car detailed."

"I'mma do better than that, I'm going to buy you a new one."

Billy gasped and told him that he was going to hold him to it.

They arrived at the mall and went in and out of every jewelry store to find the perfect gift for the women in their lives. Eventually, Billy's stomach began to growl, and they stopped at the food court. Billy ordered a Philly cheesesteak sandwich and fries but Wilt elected to have a burger without the bun, a small order of fries, and water.

"I see Brooke's gift done took all your money, huh? She got you on a diet," Billy joked. The truth was that Wilt was trying to watch his weight and wanted to build more muscle before entering the NFL draft.

"Man, whatever. I'm trying to slim down. You need to listen to yo' other woman's advice about your BMI."

"Other woman?"

"Yeah, Barbara."

Billy laughed and told Wilt that he was tripping and kept reiterating that they were *friends*. "You think men and women can't be friends?"

"Yeah, they can, but not with women who they are in love with."

Billy expressed to Wilt that he was in love with Sasha, not Barbara. The minute those words escaped his mouth, he looked at Barnes & Noble, which reminded him he had to get a gift from there. He left Wilt at the table deep in his thoughts and ran inside the store to buy a book. When he returned his Philly sandwich and fries were gone.

"What happened to my food?"

"I threw it away because I'm looking out for you."

Billy warned him that if he touched his food again he was going to be looking out for his fist upside his nugget. And he wasn't talking about any *chicken* nuggets.

"Whatever. You gon' thank me later."

Billy and Wilt's shopping spree was over, and they decided to visit a few of their classmates from high school before returning home to watch Wilt and his putt-putt smoke its way down the street. Billy swore the car was either going to die or burst into flames it was so raggedy.

Billy walked inside the house and noticed his mother's new hairdo and how she patted her hands against it, loving how she looked. She kept turning to the left and right and finally held up another mirror so she could see the back.

"Ooooweee, can I get with you?" Billy said as he came up behind her, startling her again.

"Billy, stop sneaking up behind me." she said, and then immediately asked, "How do I look?" She did a three-hundred-and-sixty-degree turn, anticipating his response.

"Mama, I can see why Daddy married you."

"Aw. Thank you, baby," she said, overjoyed.

"You look just like me."

"Get on out of here with that '*You look just like me*' mess." She laughed because it was the other way around. He changed the subject and asked where Brandy was, and his mother said she was out with Olivia. He sighed because he wanted to get her opinion on Sasha's Christmas gift.

His phone rang and it was the distraction needed to end the conversation between him and his mother. He walked to his room, closed the door, lay down on his bed, and whispered.

"Hey babe, where are you? I've been calling you all morning."

Sasha had been out shopping with her mother, but she'd lost track of time and her phone died as well. She called Billy as soon as she got home and asked if she could come over. Billy offered to pick her up, but she declined. She was driving her mom's car and only fifteen minutes away from his house. He had to jump in the shower, but said he would go and unlock the front door so she could come right in.

Brandy was in the kitchen fixing a sandwich when she heard the front door open. Earlier, she'd seen Billy run downstairs and then go up but didn't know what he was doing. Seeing Sasha walk inside, she knew he'd unlocked it. She gave Sasha the side eye and spoke reluctantly. She still had the pictures of her and dreadlocked, weed-smoking Rashad slow dancing a little too close at the club. She didn't know if he smoked but he just looked like one of those Bob Marley weed-smoking Jamaicans.

"You all right, Brandy?"

"Yeah, I'm good. And you?" Brandy had an attitude and Sasha wasn't the one to get sassy with because she got 'tude too. She decided to ignore Billy's *little* sister and head into his room to wait for him to get out of the shower. She passed by his mother's room to speak to her and complimented her hairdo. Melody showed her the dress that she bought for Christmas. "Wow. You gon' be fly, Mrs. Daye." Sasha held the hanger with the dress and pressed it against her body as if she was the one trying it on. Melody soaked it all in and couldn't wait to show it off. She had been talking to Sasha for over fifteen minutes and didn't want to hold her up any longer because she knew Billy had been waiting for her.

Billy's door was slightly ajar and Sasha saw him sitting on his bed with his sister. Brandy could no longer let Sasha play her brother, so she told him about Rashad at the club. Billy said it was nothing but a *dance.* He danced with women too when he was away at college, and he trusted Sasha. He assured Brandy that it was *nothing* as he looked at each dark photo of a baby blue dress dancing with a man that he didn't recognize. He couldn't even see Sasha or Rashad's faces. The dark lighting in the club distorted the quality of the pictures.

"I appreciate you, sis. Talk to you later." Billy hugged his sister and thanked her for trying to look out for him. She passed Sasha without a word, looking back to wish *her brother* a good night.

Billy invited Sasha over to his bed, took off her shoes, and started rubbing her feet. This always made her calm, relaxed, and horny, but not tonight. After he rubbed her feet, she decided to ask him about his relationship with her cousin.

"Babe, how long had you known Barbara before we met?" Billy didn't know where her question was going because his plan was to not talk about anyone or anything. He wanted their bodies to do all the talking and listening.

"Not long. Why?" He sighed.

"Do you like her?"

"Yeah, of course. She's your cousin. She's family. How could I not like her?" Sasha grabbed the pillow and hit him with it. "You know what I mean, stop playing dumb." She laughed, but in a serious way.

He professed his feelings for Sasha, told her he was in love with her, and that Barbara was nothing more than a friend. He wanted to prove his devotion to her that night, so he began taking off her blouse. She hesitated at first but asked him to look into her eyes and tell her the truth. She could always tell when a man lied; he would look all around instead of making eye contact. He looked into her eyes, and before the night was over, she was Billy's one and only love. *His future wife.*

Chapter Eighteen

The weather had been gloomy and cloudy but warm. It didn't feel like Christmas Day, especially for Melody. As soon as she finished eating with her children, she was called into work because one of the nurse's was ill. She accepted but said that she could only work half a shift and not the full work night. Her supervisor agreed and would try to find someone else to fill in.

"Mama, it seems like *every* year when it's your time off for Christmas, there's an "emergency" at the hospital or someone calls in. You're not the only Registered Nurse." Brandy was frustrated and wanted to spend more quality time as a family.

"Yeah, I know, but what can I do? I need my job." Melody needing her job was far from the truth. Her husband had left the family money from his investment accounts and life insurance; the house and cars were paid in full. The truth was that since her husband passed away, she wanted to spend less time at home because everything surrounding her brought back memories. The songs on the radio, the late-night walks around the neighborhood, the barbecues in their oversized backyard, and date nights. She adored only one man and it had been love at first sight. She knew when she first saw him that he would be her future husband. His athletic six-four body towered over her five-foot four average height and weight. They married two years after high school and that's when she got pregnant with Billy. Billy Sr. would hurry home to put him to bed every night and when Billy began to walk, there was a football placed in his hand. He always bragged about his son making it to the NFL. He taught Billy to throw with both hands. By the time he was thirteen years old, he could throw a spiral pass over fifty yards into the wind.

Billy Sr. would sit with Brandy and let her paint his nails all different shades of the rainbow. And when he took the polish off the next day for work, he'd come home and she would repaint them and let him know she didn't appreciate him taking it off. He was proud of both his children and his family was his life.

"Mama, what about your friend and his family that you were supposed to meet today?"

"Brandy, it's all right. I've already talked to him and told him that I would be a little late. Now, you kids finish off the dishes and don't worry about me."

"Can we at least open the gifts before you leave?" Melody agreed and they began exchanging gifts and thanking each other. Brandy and Melody both got beautiful tennis bracelets and earrings and Billy got a nice watch and Timberland boots.

Melody was off to work, and Billy and Brandy began cleaning the kitchen. They were both having Christmas dinner at Barbara's home in another three hours.

Nat King Cole's "The Christmas Song" crooned through the speakers as Sasha and Barbara were preparing Christmas dinner. They could hardly finish because of all the interruptions from Suzie and Lizzy checking in to make sure they were preparing everything correctly. Sasha began making jokes mimicking them.

"How much paprika did you put in the potato salad?"

"How long has that mac and cheese been in the oven?"

"Did you rinse the collard green three times?"

The questions were endless and Sasha's impersonation of her aunt and mother had Barbara gasping for air holding her stomach.

"What's so funny in here?" Phillip asked as he came into the kitchen catching their laughter. He held Barbara from behind, kissed her on the cheek, and whispered in her ear. "You know I love you, right?"

"You better," she teased.

"Y'all need to get a room," Sasha recommended playfully. Phillip couldn't agree more but he respected Barbara too much. He asked if they needed anything before he left the kitchen, but they had already sent him twice to the store for more milk, eggs, and butter.

Sasha's cell phone rang, and she answered after the third ring. Barbara noticed the letters **RL** on the phone display. She knew it was Rashad Lewis because Sasha told him to hold and went into another room for privacy. She came back five minutes later smiling and Barbara was annoyed with Sasha because she liked Billy as a friend and didn't like how her cousin was seeing both Billy and Rashad.

"How long are you going to string Billy along?"

Sasha wasn't *stringing* Billy along. She loved him, but Rashad was unique and brought out a different side of her. Rashad had a wild daredevil side to him that excited her, and Billy was just Billy Daye, a football player.

"Why is it any of *your* business? Billy is *my* man." Barbara didn't know whether to ignore her and keep the peace or push harder. It was Christmas, but she was tired of Sasha's deceitful ways, and she didn't want to lie anymore about her whereabouts. For the past two weeks Sasha has been with Rashad, telling her family and Billy that she was with Barbara.

"Sasha, Billy is my friend and he's a good guy. He doesn't deserve what you are doing to him."

"And what am I doing to him? Huh? Like I said, he's my man. My future husband, not yours, so get over this *little* crush that you have on him."

"Wait a minute? Is that what you think? You got it all wrong. I'm his friend and I care about him." Sasha didn't believe it. She knew Barbara cared for Billy more than she wanted her to know. She saw the way they looked at each other, not to mention the kiss a few weeks ago. She wasn't about to get left out in the dark, and that was the reason she had become closer to Rashad.

Another interruption turned the conversation in a much calmer direction when Leon walked into the kitchen singing Christmas songs. He couldn't sing a lick. In fact, the only time he sang was during the Christmas season. It brought out the joy in him, but also everyone else. He sang, performing the Temptations' "Silent Night."

He asked Sasha and Barbara to sing with him. They looked at each other and knew Leon was not going to stop until he had background singers. So, they began to sing along. And into the kitchen walked Suzie and Lizzy to join them, even though they secretly were in there to check on dinner again. Before anyone knew it, all the guests were in the kitchen either getting snacks or singing.

The doorbell rang and Barbara offered to get it. As she walked to the door, Phillip walked up behind her. She opened the door and there stood Billy Daye looking more handsome than ever. His smile disappeared once he saw Phillip come up to gently hug Barbara. Brandy was inside the car getting a cake she'd made and walked up to see the exchange. Billy and Barbara looked into each other's eyes like they were in a trance. Brandy moved her brother out of the way to enter first as Barbara and Phillip stepped to the side in unison.

"Hey, Bill Daye," a familiar voice came from behind Billy. He turned and wanted to punch Kurt in his face for continuing to call him *Bill*.

"Who's this clown?" Kurt asked as he saw Phillip with his arms around Barbara. She introduced Phillip to Billy and Kurt. Billy shook Phillip's hand, but Kurt ignored it and asked Barbara where to put the vegetarian dish he'd made. She took it out of his hands and thanked him. He held a mistletoe over her head and she laughed. "I know you didn't."

He immediately kissed her on the cheek even though he was aiming for her lips. Thankfully she turned her face. Phillip didn't like what he saw and immediately thought to himself, *public enemy number one*. He faked a smile and showed Billy and Kurt to the area where the guys were hanging out waiting for dinner. In the man cave, they watched the NBA and played dominoes and poker.

Billy had his eyes on Phillip, but Kurt watched Phillip *and* Billy. Billy saw Phillip's schoolboy demeanor and the way he adjusted his glasses. He was handsome, but of course he couldn't compare to Billy. He checked him out from head to toe, subconsciously comparing himself to Phillip. If it wasn't for a text message jarring him away from Phillip, he'd still be analyzing him. It was from Wilt letting him know that he and Brooke were on their way over.

Brandy was in the kitchen assisting Barbara and Sasha. She let them know that Olivia would be over after she had dinner with her family. Sasha asked about Billy, not knowing he 'd just arrived. She went into the man cave and gave him a big hug and kiss, and sat upon his lap. She spoke to Kurt and wished him a Merry Christmas. He still had the mistletoe in his hand, but it wasn't for Sasha, it was for Barbara. Even though Billy silently dared him to try it with Sasha because he wanted to punch him for that incident earlier with Barbara. He needed a legitimate excuse. Kurt knew where to draw the line so he sat back and began conversing with Leon.

Two hours later, dinner was ready, and everyone was famished. It took a lot longer than when Suzie and Lizzy prepared Christmas supper. In fact, it took more time because Barbara and Sasha had to compromise and remake dishes to appease them. The food looked and smelled good, and according to everyone, it was delicious. Soon after eating the kitchen was cleaned, and it was time for the opening of the gifts.

Billy handed a small box to Sasha as he got down on one knee. Lizzy brought her hands to her mouth and Jimmy held her tight. It was the day their daughter was going to be engaged. Sasha was elated and could hardly wait to open the neatly-wrapped gift. But inside was a forever white-gold shiny necklace. It was a nice gift but a huge disappointment because Sasha and her parents thought it would be an engagement ring. Sasha masked her disappointment and kissed and thanked her man for it. He then gave Barbara a gift and even she was shocked because she didn't get him anything.

"Billy, I can't accept this because I didn't get you anything."

"Don't be silly. I've owed you this for years."

She reluctantly accepted as Phillip and everyone else looked on to see what was inside. She unwrapped the gift and pulled out a book, *Tar Baby*. She began to laugh hysterically after reading the card inside. *"I wanted to replace your book that you left at the bus stop years ago when I had to protect you from Jeffrey Dahmer. Billy Daye."*

A tear dropped from her eyes because she couldn't believe that after all these years, he still remembered that she lost her book. Wilt looked at Billy and thought to himself, *that's why he made that trip to the bookstore when we went to the mall*. He knew his best friend had the hots for Barbara. Sasha rolled her eyes because her thoughts were the same as Wilt's.

Barbara hugged and thanked Billy, but this was immediately interrupted as Kurt handed her his gift. She opened it and it was her original *Tar Baby* book that he found at the bus stop but never got around to giving to her.

"Now, this here is your original book, with all the notes and highlights."

Leon shook his head side to side at how these men were trying to get his daughter's attention. Phillip cleared his throat and asked for everyone's attention. He asked them to pour themselves a glass of wine, then walked to where his jacket was hanging and retrieved Barbara's gift out of the pocket.

He first handed her a card which she opened and read, but then she began to shake. Phillip got down on one knee and handed her the small wrapped box. She dropped it because she was nervous and shaking with excitement. She opened the Tiffany & Co. box and there sat a sparkling two carat Tiffany diamond engagement ring.

"Barbara Knight, will you make me the happiest man in the world by being my wife?"

"Hell, to the naw." Kurt shouted. He didn't give Barbara a chance to answer, and Phillip being a nice guy, tried to ignore Kurt. But he wouldn't stop talking. Billy, for once, didn't want him to either. Everyone waited for her answer as she looked directly into Billy's eyes. He nodded his head as she looked at him, the ring, and Phillip. She had to decide. Phillip was still down on one knee when the doorbell rang.

Leon went to answer, and as he opened the door, a woman walked inside without being invited. Leon almost passed out. He couldn't take any more of her nonsense. Especially on Christmas Day.

"Where the hell is my daughter? I came to see my daughter." She began calling her name. "Barbara, where are you?" As soon as Barbara accepted Phillip's proposal, she heard her mother calling her. Lizzy jumped up immediately to stop Jenny.

"Lizzy, if you don't get the hell out of my way. I swear I will tell it all."

"Mama, what is it? What are you doing?" Barbara asked.

"I'm here to tell you everything." Leon tried to stop Jenny, but she was furious and it was time for everyone to know the truth. Suzie began talking to Jenny, trying to calm her down and begging her not to do this on Christmas Day.

"I don't give a damn about it being Christmas. I tried calling her and texting her but didn't get a response. Today I came to tell my daughter what she needs to know." Jimmy tried to interrupt but she told him that he better sit his black ass down somewhere and not to touch her.

Phillip didn't know who Jenny was and held his fiancée tight. Jenny saw the diamond ring on her daughter's hand and began asking Phillip who he was.

"Mom, this is Phillip, my fiancé. He asked me to marry him, and I accepted." Jenny calmed down for a second and congratulated them both. She saw the joy in her daughter's eyes. And then she went on another tirade as if she was suffering from bipolar.

Leon pulled Jenny to the side and whispered in her ear. "Ten thousand deposited into your bank account by tomorrow morning."

She thought about his words for a second while Lizzy and Jimmy nervously looked on, then she whispered back to Leon: "Not a chance in hell."

Lizzy told Jimmy she wanted to talk to him in private. They walked into another room and she began asking him how Jenny could be back again. "I thought you took care of her? She's going to ruin everything." He tried to calm his wife down and said he didn't know what happened and that he would get to the bottom of it. "You better. She's a ticking time bomb."

"Everyone, please be quiet and let Aunt Jenny speak." Sasha shouted through all the commotion.

On that note, Jenny began telling Barbara how she and Leon met, and that he was her first love. They did everything together and never held any secrets until they broke up and Lizzy slept with Leon. Soon after, Jenny found out about her boyfriend's deceit, and she slept with Lizzy's man, Jimmy. Leon and Jenny got back together, and soon after they got married. She found out that she was pregnant and knew there was a slight chance it could be Jimmy's child. Leon and Lizzy had no idea about Jenny and Jimmy until years later when they got into a big argument and Lizzy told Jenny that she had slept with Leon and Sasha was his biological daughter. This was the reason Jenny left years ago. She was devastated.

"Mama, what is Aunt Jenny talking about?" Sasha turned to her mother for an explanation.

Barbara looked at her father and asked if it was true. The look on his face said it all. She began hysterically crying and saying to him, "Dad, how could you do this to me?" Phillip held her close as she cried into his arms.

"Oh, that's not the end, baby. Jimmy is your biological father, not Leon." Barbara couldn't take any more. She grabbed her car keys and began rushing out the door to get away from it all. *Her Uncle Jimmy was her father, and her father was her Uncle Leon?*

Phillip was in hot pursuit as he ran after her and so was Billy. When they got to the front door, Billy's mother Melody pulled up to the front of the home. She got out of her car and saw a young woman crying and Billy and another guy running after her.

"Mama, what are you doing here?"

"What do you mean, what am I doing here? I'm at my friend's home. The one I told you about."

"Leon, is your friend? The one you've been getting your groove on with?"

"Well, yes, he's my friend but..."

Billy stopped her and said she couldn't date Leon. He told her to get in the car and leave right away, and said he would explain everything when he got home.

"Billy, what? Why?"

"Mama, please just do what I asked you to do."

She did what her son asked. She got into the car and went home without going inside to tell Leon that she had arrived.

Billy opened Barbara's car door and got inside while Phillip tried to stop her. He lost his balance and fell to the ground. He'd injured his back and couldn't move. Barbara was so distraught she didn't notice Phillip on the ground, though she knew he had a bad back. She saw Billy get into her car and didn't object. She just wanted to get away.

"Barbara, pull over and let me take the wheel. You are in no condition to drive." She kept speeding even faster as he pleaded with her. "Please pull over before you kill us both."

Ten miles to nowhere later, she pulled over and let Billy drive. He said nothing as he got into the driver's seat and she cried into the passenger's seat. They drove out of San Antonio toward Austin with no destination in mind. They pulled into the Hilton Hotel parking lot because they had been driving for over an hour. Emotions were high and they were both exhausted.

"Do you want to stay here for the night and head back home in the morning?" he asked.

"Home? Where is home? There is no home. My life is nothing but lies, Billy." She began to cry even more thinking about her reality.

"It's going to be all right. I know it's a lot to take in, but you *need* some rest. Let me go pay for two separate rooms. I'll be right back." Billy got out of the car and asked the hotel attendant for two rooms, but unfortunately, they only had one available. He paid for it and decided that he would sleep out in the car as long as Barbara was safe. He walked back and gave her the key to the hotel room, telling her about the room situation.

"You don't have to sleep in the car. It's okay to share a room. Doesn't it have two beds?"

"No, there's only one queen-size bed and a chair."

"Well, you can take the chair. I won't have you sleeping out in the car. It's too small and you will be uncomfortable."

"Are you sure? Because you know I'm not afraid of Mr. Dahmer." Every time he made a joke about Jeffrey Dahmer, Barbara laughed, and Billy doing his greatest Muhammad Ali impression to show her how he would handle the mass murderer made her laugh even harder and forget about her troubles in San Antonio.

"Yes, I'm sure. Now, would you come on?" She opened the trunk of her car. Thankfully she hadn't taken all her bags inside the day she last went shopping. She'd bought a nice dress, booty shorts and tank top, along with underwear and bras from Victoria's Secret. She'd also bought Phillip a nice shirt and shorts. She grabbed the bag and playfully took Billy's hand as they found Room #202.

The room was cozy and romantic, it was perfect for *couples*, except Barbara and Billy weren't together. They were friends looking out for one another. He let her use the bathroom first as she showered and put on her tank top and booty shorts. She walked out of the bathroom and Billy couldn't help but notice her figure eight physique. He turned his head so she wouldn't catch him staring as he continued watching SportsCenter. She pulled out Phillip's shirt and shorts and gave them to Billy so that he could shower and get dressed.

"Naw, I'm good. I'm not about to put on another man's clothing."

"Technically, they are brand new."

"Yeah, but they were not meant for me, and they look too small for these guns." He pumped his arms and chest. She rolled her eyes and told him to put them on, now. "Dang, okay. Okay. You're getting a little bossy," he teased.

"Go get in the shower." She pointed at the bathroom door. He did what he was told and while he was in the shower, she thought to herself that she wasn't going to watch SportsCenter all night. She flipped through the channels on the TV until she found the movie, *Love And Basketball* with Sana Lathan and Omar Epps. She wished she had some popcorn and soda.

When Billy got out of the shower, the shirt and shorts she gave him fit a little tight, but it wasn't too bad. Billy thought he looked like the sucker she had just gotten engaged to. He walked out of the bathroom doing a nerd impression of Phillip. Barbara laughed and asked if he would go and get her a snack while she watched the movie.

Billy went to the vending machine and there was an area that had freshly-popped popcorn. He grabbed a couple of bags and brought back chips and soda too. He even had Boston Baked Beans candies. Barbara was excited and couldn't believe he found fresh hot buttered popcorn. She lay in the bed and Billy sat in the chair enjoying the movie. She saw him shift side to side trying to get comfortable and she patted the bed and told him to come lay down.

"Naw, I'm good." He refused because he didn't want to invade the little privacy she had. She continued to tell him it was okay and she didn't feel right being comfortable while he sat in the chair trying to find different positions to relax. "Barbara, how would your fiancé feel about me in the same bed as you? Not to mention, *my* girlfriend, your *cousin*, Sasha?"

"Phillip is not like that. He is understanding and he knows me."

"And what about Sasha? You know she has asked about our *friendship* a few times."

There was nothing to worry about, Barbara assured him. They were just watching a movie together and nothing more. Billy reluctantly got into the bed and drew an imaginary line telling her to stay on her side of the bed while he stayed on his.

Two hours later, the movie ended, and Barbara was sound asleep. Billy turned the TV back to SportsCenter so he could see the score between the Spurs and Bulls. He watched Barbara lightly snore and move around in her sleep. Her leg was well past the imaginary line he drew earlier. He looked at every inch of her leg leading up to her behind. *Damn, she has a nice body,* he thought to himself, but her heart was what he admired the most. He took his hand and reached to put the blanket over her body and turned his attention back to the TV. He was not only a good friend, but the perfect gentleman.

Chapter Nineteen

Rashad and Sasha pulled into the Hilton Hotel where he had rented a room for a DJ gig he had in Austin. She was very upset about Christmas Day and told him how her uncle was her biological father and her stepfather was her cousin's biological dad. And how her man ran after her cousin and left with *her*. She knew Billy was in love with Barbara but didn't want to admit it.

"That's messed up," Rashad kept reiterating as Sasha cried and kept wondering how this had happened.

Rashad got out of the car first and went around to open the door for Sasha. He grabbed her suitcase with her personal items and held her hand as they walked up the stairs to Room #204.

When they reached the top of the stairs, they heard laughter. That's when they saw Billy and Barbara giggling with the door open to Room #202. They were laughing about his mother and Leon getting their groove on. Sasha didn't know whether to confront them or not because she was there with a suitcase in her hand with another man. It was the case of the song "I Was Checking Out, She Was Checking In" by Don Covay. The song is about a married man cheating on his wife with a married woman. While he was waiting in the parking lot of a hotel, he saw his wife checking into the same hotel with another man. But he couldn't say anything because he was cheating too.

Sasha grabbed Rashad and pulled him back to the stairs and out of sight of Barbara and Billy.

"Do you want something to drink before we leave?" Sasha heard Billy ask Barbara. She couldn't hear her response because Billy and Barbara walked directly into the stairwell and saw Rashad and Sasha who stood behind him in a hiding position. Billy couldn't believe his eyes. In fact, he thought it was a nightmare he needed to wake up from, and quickly.

"Sasha, what are you doing?"

"What the hell do you mean, what am I doing? The question is what are you doing here with my cousin?" Barbara tried to explain to Sasha that it was not even like that and she knew it. But she also knew that Sasha was cheating on Billy with Rashad, and from her point of view, it was Sasha that was in the wrong.

"Man, what are you doing with my woman?" Billy asked Rashad as he tried to remove his hand from Sasha's. Rashad told Billy not to touch him and said it looked like Sasha wasn't his woman since he was seen coming out of a hotel room with her *cousin*. Billy stood man to man in Rashad's face with his fists balled and chest towering over Rashad's five-foot-ten body frame.

"Man, you better back up off of me." Rashad warned Billy as Barbara grabbed Billy's arm trying to escort him down the stairs, telling him it wasn't worth it. Billy squeezed his fists even tighter and his lips began to quiver, but Rashad wasn't backing down either until Sasha grabbed him and said, "Let's go."

"Billy, it's over. You can have her. I can't compete any longer and I give up."

"Compete with who, Sasha? Barbara and I are just friends."

"Oh yeah? Then why are you here with her instead of comforting me, huh? I heard the same news she did, but you ran off with her and you never even called to check up on me." Sasha cried tears of sadness and anger.

"Baby, I'm sorry. Everything happened so fast."

"Yeah, it did. But your actions told me who you wanted to be with, so move out of my way. It's over Billy."

"Sasha, don't do this. Can we go somewhere and talk in private?" Sasha refused. She took Rashad's hand and led him where they were headed before they saw Billy and Barbara. Billy watched in dismay and called out her name. She pretended not to hear him as Rashad slid the card key and unlocked the room. They both walked inside and closed the door. Billy watched as Barbara held his arm, asking him to leave and saying it was going to be all right.

The car ride was silent as Barbara drove to IHOP. Billy held his hand over his face to cover his tears. He looked down at his cell phone and noticed eight missed calls, all from his mother and sister. He scrolled to his contact list, and under "B" were his sister, Brandy, Barbara, and *Babe* meaning Sasha. He pulled up "Babe" and swiped, choosing to delete the contact. He put his phone back in his pocket and cried silently into his hands.

Ten minutes later they were at the restaurant and Barbara asked Billy if he was okay. He assured her he was, and that it was better to know the truth than have your woman cheating with another man behind your back. The waiter came to take their order and Billy wanted the grand slam breakfast and so did Barbara. Except he added sausage and she gave him hers.

"Can I ask you a question?"

"Do I have a choice?" Barbara asked.

"No, not really. Did you know that Sasha was cheating on me?"

Barbara didn't want to answer. She thought for a minute as she took a sip of her ice-cold water. Billy waited for an answer that he wasn't ready to accept.

"Yes, unfortunately. But I tried to talk to her and she wouldn't listen. She thought that you and I had a thing for each other—"

Billy stopped her mid-sentence, wanting to know how long Sasha had been cheating. Barbara told him how she met Rashad the night they went to open mic. Billy shook his head because he couldn't believe he trusted her and thought back to all the times she didn't answer her phone and made excuses on how she left it at home, or it was dead from not charging it. He couldn't believe he'd been a sucker for another woman like Lisa who broke his heart. He thought to himself, *when will I ever learn?* Billy hardly ate his breakfast, in fact, he did more thinking than eating, and so did Barbara.

"Are you ready to go back home?" Billy asked to change the melancholy mood that he was in and get his mind off Sasha and Rashad.

"No, I'm not going back home. In fact, I might stay here and find me an apartment and get a job."

"What? Barbara, I think you owe it to your father to hear him out and then decide what you are going to do. Besides, what about Phillip?"

"Maybe. But he had the opportunity to tell me years ago and he didn't. I should have put two and two together when he was in the car accident and my blood type didn't match his, but Sasha's did." She caught herself. She hadn't intended to bring up Sasha's name, so she instantly agreed that they should head back home and hear Leon's side of the story. She wanted to call Phillip too, but she'd left her cell phone at home when she ran out the door and didn't want to use Billy's phone to call him.

Billy agreed that whatever decision she made, he would help her and be by her side *if* she needed him. He didn't want to overstep his boundaries because she had her man, but he didn't want to lose her friendship either. He reiterated, *Barbara has a man, but I am single, again.* He sighed and wondered how he was going to tell Wilt that he had been played like a deck of cards.

After dropping Billy off at home, Barbara pulled in her driveway and saw Leon taking the trash bin to the back of the house. He looked unshaven, bum-like, and tired, as if he hadn't slept in years. He saw her and hugged her tight.

"Pumpkin, I'm so glad you are home. I was so worried about you."

"Where's Phillip?" She asked as she reluctantly embraced him.

"He left about an hour ago, headed back to Houston. He said he tried to call you, but your phone was left here. You should call him as soon as possible to let him know that you are safe."

Leon opened the front door and let Barbara walk in first. The Christmas tree had been taken down and all the decorations were gone. Barbara thought back to Christmas Day when her mom came to tell her the truth, and how happy she'd been before she arrived. Now her world was confused, uncertain, and she had so many questions. She took a seat on the sofa and Leon sat next to her. He began telling her *everything* about how he didn't know that she wasn't his daughter until she was ten years old, and he wasn't going to give her up because he loved her too much. He explained that he also didn't know Sasha was his daughter until Christmas Day. Lizzy had kept it a secret from him but told Jenny and she went ballistic. That was the reason she ran off with another man.

"I wasn't willing to give you up for nothing in the world, so Lizzy and Jimmy paid your mother money to keep quiet. But she kept wanting more money."

Leon grabbed Barbara's hand to explain to her that he didn't even know Jimmy was her father until Christmas Day. The only person who knew was Jenny. Lizzy didn't know and neither did Jimmy. He thought he was paying off Jenny for her Aunt Lizzy's sake.

"Wait a minute, so you mean to tell me that Uncle Jimmy didn't even know I was his daughter?"

"No, he didn't, not until the other day."

Barbara thought back to the night she stayed at Sasha's house. She'd seen Jimmy leave in the middle of the night when her mother was in town and then her mother had disappeared and didn't show up for their girls' day out.

"So, where do we go from here, Da..?" She stopped herself because she didn't know whether to call him Dad or Leon.

"Sweetheart. We pick up from where we left off. Nothing has changed. My love for you is *unconditional*." Barbara began to cry hearing those words. She knew her dad loved her, but she hated the fact that the same blood didn't run through her veins as his. He softly placed his arms around her and held her tight.

"Dad, there's one more thing I need to ask you."

"What is it?"

"The night you had the car accident, did you try to kill yourself?" Leon was taken aback because his accident had been over four years ago. He didn't understand why Barbara was asking him about it now. He hesitated but realized he needed to be open with her or risk losing her for good. He sighed and began telling her how he was on his way to the hospital to check on Amber's condition and received a phone call from Jenny. He met with her, they got into an argument, and she was the cause of his accident.

"Jenny told the policeman that I tried to kill myself and she tried to stop me. But the truth was, she wanted more money and was threatening to tell you that I wasn't your father."

It really stung when he said, *he wasn't her father* but Leon went on to say that he was her dad, and he wouldn't let DNA take that obligation nor right away from him. *He was her father.*

"I love you, Dad."

"I love you more than life, Pumpkin. Now, please go and give Phillip a call."

Barbara went upstairs and sat down on the bed. She thought about all the events that had taken place from Christmas Day until earlier that day, seeing Sasha and Rashad at the hotel room. She picked up her cell phone and listened to all the messages Phillip left on Christmas. She smiled and thought about how lucky she was to have such a caring and wonderful man. She looked at her ring and held her hand out. This was the first time she was able to admire it and think about marrying the man of her dreams. Her life was finally making sense and there were no more secrets.

She dialed Phillip's cell phone and he answered immediately. She couldn't get one word in. He was so happy to hear from her and couldn't stop telling her how much he loved her. She could hear the heavy traffic in the background and then suddenly a loud honk and a crash, and Phillip's call ended. She immediately called back but there was no answer, only his voicemail. She called and called to no avail. She began to panic and that's when her dad ran upstairs to see what was wrong with her.

"It's Phillip, I think he's been in an accident. I have to get to him." Leon offered to go along with her because she was in no condition to drive. He grabbed the keys to his car and decided to take it. Barbara prayed and cried, hoping her fiancé was okay, but knew in her heart that it wasn't good. She'd heard a loud horn from an eighteen-wheeler truck and then a crash as Phillip's phone died. Leon tried to calm her down as best as he could and assure her that he was probably okay. But she blamed herself for calling him while he was on the road. This was something that she would never do normally because she didn't want him distracted.

One hundred miles down the road, you could hear sirens and lights from police cars, an ambulance, and the fire department. As they got closer, she could see an eighteen-wheeler rig turned upside down and a car underneath it smashed like a pancake. She began to scream when she recognized that it was Phillip's car. As Leon slowed down, Barbara jumped out of the car without notice and ran to the wrecked car. She heard concerned onlookers saying that it was fatal and there was no way the person in the car could have survived. Barbara began calling his name and a policeman tried to remove her from the scene.

"Get your hands off me. He's my fiancé."

"I'm sorry ma'am, but we can't let you through. Do you know his next of kin?" Barbara sobbed because she had never met Phillip's parents. She had only talked to them via telephone.

She didn't speak, she couldn't. She just screamed at the top of her lungs. Leon came from behind her to take her away from the scene.

"No. Daddy, why?" She wanted to know why every time she was about to be so happy, something would happen to ruin it. Leon didn't answer. He held her like a child as he rubbed her back and walked her to the car.

"Daddy, no, I want to see him."

"Barbara, honey, that's not a good idea. I have to get you back to the car."

She refused to leave until she saw Phillip, but when she did, a black bag had covered his entire body. She cried louder into her father's arms.

"Pumpkin, let's go. This is not good for you to see."

Her anguish was so extreme that it brought tears to Leon's eyes. He too had to hold it together because he admired Phillip and was looking forward to him being his son-in-law. But the day after Christmas, his young life was gone, and his daughter would have to cope with the pain of his absence. To cope with what would have, should have, or could have been had she not called him at that moment.

Chapter Twenty

Billy was drafted tenth overall to the Washington Redskins but unfortunately Wilt went undrafted. He was invited to several NFL teams' tryouts and was hoping to make the practice squad. Moving to Washington, DC wasn't Billy's preference, but he knew it was a privilege being in the National Football League. He asked Wilt to move to Washington with him so he could be his agent.

"Fo' real. You're going to put me on your payroll like that?"

"Yeah, why not? You know a lot about contracts, and you have a marketing degree."

"I don't know, man. You know I got my girl and everything and she *might* be pregnant."

"Pregnant? Man, you're crazy for not using protection." Billy began scolding him about bringing children into this world without a direct career path and how it adds stress to a relationship. He started thinking about Sasha and how she played him like a fiddle, and thanked God a child didn't come from that relationship. He still thought about her from time to time and even saw her with Rashad a few weeks ago, but she seemed content, and he was happy she was being treated well. He wished her nothing but the best with school and getting her law degree.

"Oh yeah, I saw your ex last week," Wilt said as if he was reading Billy's mind. "She looked better after the tragedy of losing her fiancé."

Billy didn't correct Wilt about Barbara being his ex because she wasn't. He held her in a special place of endearment in his heart and had visited her almost daily since Phillip's death. He attended the burial along with her and Leon. He accompanied her to her therapy sessions and kept reiterating that she wasn't to blame for the accident. The truck driver's blood-alcohol level was three times higher than the legal amount. It was like Joshua's level when he crashed into Billy's father and killed him that fateful day. He assured Barbara that time would help her cope with the loss.

She continued to wear the engagement ring and cherish the memories, although Billy felt she needed to put it in a safe deposit box and move on with her life. Her therapist recommended the opposite, encouraging her to take as much time as she needed to heal and assuring her there was no time limit for lamenting.

"My ex? Naw, she's still in my life and will be forever," Billy replied to Wilt.

"See, I knew you were in love with her. Y'all need to just go on and get married. I'm tellin' you, bro. You've been into her since high school."

Billy smashed his domino on the table and shouted, "Domino with twenty-five." Wilt laughed because that was the third game, and Billy had won them all. Billy considered himself a *dominologist* and Wilt couldn't disagree. If he hadn't known his best friend all his life, he would have thought he'd gone to prison and played dominos during his entire bid. People who'd been in prison were the best at dominos.

"So, what are you doing tomorrow?" Wilt asked.

"Nothing. Probably going to check on Barbara and then start packing. Why, what's up?"

"Brooke wants me to attend her friend's wedding with her and you know I don't want her getting any ideas. Because I ain't ready for no ball and chain. It ain't happening."

"Wait, didn't you just say that she 'might' be pregnant?"

"Yeah, but that don't mean nothing."

"What you mean, that don't mean nothing? Wilt, you better handle your responsibility if she *is* pregnant. And if not, you better start wrapping up that little dip stick of yours." Billy took his thumb and index finger and placed them about an inch apart to demonstrate the length of Wilt's penis. Wilt began laughing as Billy cracked a joke about how they couldn't find a jock strap to fit him when they were in middle school. "Yeah, that's because of this anaconda."

"Man, please."

They heard the door to the patio open and it was Melody looking and smelling nice. "Mama, where are you going looking all good?"

"I got some errands to run and then I'll be back to cook supper. Wilt, are you going to be here later?" Wilt could never turn down his second mom's food, so he told her to save him a seat at the table. She smiled because she knew his answer but loved receiving accolades for her home cooking.

"Mama, I'm going to invite Barbara, and yeah, Leon is cool too."

Melody didn't know whether to invite Leon or not after the incident on Christmas day. She had decided they would remain friends with no benefits and she hadn't been seeing him like before. She knew Billy didn't accept them dating, even though he left the decision up to her. But Brandy vehemently discouraged the relationship. She felt there was too much drama between Leon and his estranged wife and didn't want her mother involved. Before she returned to school, she made it clear and often called to make sure Leon was nowhere around.

"All right, Mama. Remember, Barbara doesn't eat meat." Melody knew this because he talked to her about Barbara one night and how much she meant to him. This was the first girl he'd had a conversation with his mother about. She'd met Lisa and Sasha, but as far as she could remember, he didn't talk about them as much as Barbara Knight. She knew she was special to her son.

After Melody left, Wilt continued asking Billy about the following day.

"So, will you chauffeur me to the wedding tomorrow?"

Billy shrugged and asked what time, saying he didn't want to put on another suit and tie. He was more comfortable in jeans, a polo and Timberlands. But he couldn't let his boi down and reluctantly agreed to attend.

Billy pulled out his phone to call Barbara. She answered on the third ring and he invited her to dinner. She really wasn't in the mood, but he threatened to come with his chainsaw and lift her out of bed and carry her. She couldn't turn him down no matter how much she tried. He cracked a few jokes to make her laugh and said he would pick her up around six.

"Man, I'm tellin' you. You are in love," Wilt continued to say as he walked out the front door. He was getting in his putt-putt to take Brooke to the hair and nail salon in time to be back at six.

"Man, as soon as I get my first check, we are going to get you a new car." Billy yelled at Wilt, but he couldn't hear because of the loud static bass coming from his speakers. Billy coughed from the exhaust and went inside.

Leon knocked on Barbara's bedroom door and asked if she wanted to go out to get something to eat. She told him about her plans with Billy and he wasn't surprised. Billy had been by his daughter's side ever since they met at Spaghetti Warehouse, even though he had been dating Sasha. He knew then how much he cared for her. He also got to know Billy's mother and knew Billy would be the *perfect* man for his daughter. He asked if he could talk to her for a minute and she obliged. She scooted over and let him take a seat on her bed.

"You know, I'm not trying to be all up in your personal life, but I can't help but notice Billy's demeanor when he's around you." Barbara was shocked that her dad would be talking this way about Billy when she had just lost her fiancé four months ago, but she sat there and listened without interrupting. Leon continued to explain how Billy looked at her the same way he used to look at her mother, and how he could tell when a man was in love.

"Oh, Dad, why does *everyone* think Billy and I are more than friends?" She sighed. He had been her cousin's man, and her relationship with Sasha had never been the same, even though Sasha called from time to time to check on her after Phillip's death. Sasha still treated Leon like an uncle and not a father. Barbara hadn't spoken to Jimmy either, though he'd tried reaching out to her on many occasions, because in her heart nothing had changed but the truth.

Leon knew deep down inside that Barbara cared more about Billy than she was willing to admit. He noticed how he made her smile and how playful she was when he was around. He had never seen her act like a giggly schoolgirl when dating Phillip. Her conversations with Billy were different. She consistently laughed, even after she hung up the phone. Leon noticed her engagement ring had been removed from her finger and didn't want to ask, but it appeared his daughter was moving on and her plans with Billy could be the reason. He didn't press any further. He decided to sit back and let it all play out, but he could predict the outcome.

When Leon was about to exit Barbara's room, he saw her phone ring and noticed Jenny's number on the caller ID. Leon left the room and Barbara closed the door for privacy. He wanted to eavesdrop on her conversation because he didn't know what Jenny was up to. He wished she would go away because it wasn't the perfect timing for her antics.

Jenny wanted to meet with Barbara. She had some important news to share and asked to see her that evening, but Barbara said she had plans. She insisted that if it was urgent she could break them, but Jenny said not to do that and they could meet the next day. Barbara agreed. She told her mother goodnight and began getting dressed for dinner at the Daye's home.

Melody was singing and cooking and the house smelled great. Billy came downstairs to join her and stuck his finger inside a pot where she was making the sauce. She popped his hand and he quickly jerked it back. She smiled because in another week her son would be leaving for Washington and it would be just her, and she would have no one to cook for. So even though she popped his hand, she enjoyed his humor, candor, and company. He was beginning to look more and more like his father, too. Billy kissed her on the cheek and told her to "cut it out." She was going to make him fat before he got to training camp. He offered to move her to DC with him but she reiterated that her home was right there in Texas. Her husband was there and she wasn't leaving him, even though Billy felt it was a good idea for her to leave and start over. He loved his father, but he wasn't coming back, and his mother was too young to be all alone. She still "had it going on and *she* looked like *him*," he'd often tell her.

"Mama, how long until the food is ready?"

"About another hour."

"All right. I'm going to pick up Barbara. If Wilt comes by before I get back, have him wait in the game room and not my room. He loves 'borrowing' stuff and I won't know until he's wearing it." Melody agreed. She had known Wilt since he was knee high to a grasshopper and she used to go to school with his parents.

"How are his mother and father?" Melody inquired.

"Trying to get their life together. I heard his father has a new lawyer who may be able to bring new evidence to his case and have him retried."

Melody shook her head because Wilt Sr. could have made something out of his life and so could Erika. It was a shame to see them get hooked on drugs and the streets. She was thankful Wilt didn't follow in their footsteps.

"Have any of the teams he tried out for called him back?"

"Naw, not yet. I offered him a job as my agent and asked him to move to DC with me, but he's thinking about it because he may have a baby on the way." Melody shook her head and prayed that wasn't the case. Wilt had his whole life ahead of him and having a child could deter him from his career. She felt he was too young and immature to have a child and needed a lot more growing up himself. Melody told Billy to make sure he was using protection because she wasn't ready to be a grandmother any time soon.

"Mama, you know me better than that. I'm still a virgin."

"Boy if you don't get out of here with that mess." She threw a handkerchief at him, and on that note, he was out the door and on his way, to pick up Barbara.

Billy pulled up to Barbara's house fifteen minutes later and saw Leon mowing the lawn. He got out of the car and Leon thanked him for looking after his daughter and said how much it meant to them both. He thought that Barbara should be ready and told him to go inside. Billy walked in and didn't see her. He took two steps at a time to get to her room. The door was slightly ajar, but he still didn't see her. He walked in and noticed the football he had given her years ago. He picked it up and smiled, but before he could put it back, Barbara came up behind him and scared the living daylights out of him. He was startled because he was snooping around in *her* room.

"Hey, you," he said as he turned around and saw the most beautiful woman in the world. Her angelic smile captured his soul. He didn't know what it was about Barbara that took his breath away. He breathed deep and took in her scent, attire, and hourglass figure. He noticed the engagement ring missing from her left hand too. He thought maybe she'd finally decided to put it in a safe deposit box so she could move on, but he didn't question it. It felt good to see her in better spirits.

"So, are you ready to go?" he asked.

"Yeah, but how do I look?" She did a three sixty spin and then smacked her lips to make sure her Mac lip gloss covered the inner corners of her full mouth.

"Aww. Do that spin move one more time," Billy joked as he kept insisting she repeat it.

"What? You're trying to make me dizzy so I fall?"

He wasn't, but he was there to catch her if she did. "Naw. I'm just trying to give you an honest opinion, so I needed a repeat of that move you just did." Barbara tapped his shoulder and told him, "Let's go." She walked out of the room first and he gave her enough space to take in all her beauty and curves. He thought to himself, *Is this normal to be attracted to my friend? My ex's cousin?* Barbara stopped and Billy kept walking, bumping right into her butt. She felt his hands grab her waist and she didn't know what to think because this was unfamiliar territory. He apologized profusely, but she blew it off. "Don't be silly. It was an accident." She knew he didn't do it on purpose.

She bid her dad farewell and told him not to worry about cooking for her because she would eat before she got home. She didn't tell him she was going to Billy's for dinner because she knew his relationship with Melody had been placed on hold since Christmas.

Billy opened her car door, and as he was going around to the driver's side, he saw Kurt running up to Barbara's side of the car. He asked how she was doing and if he could come by later that night. She acknowledged that she was doing much better, and of course he could come and visit her *later*. Billy didn't want to be rude, so he let Kurt finish his conversation and then they were on their way to *his* house.

"What do you see in that guy?" Billy was irritated by him, especially knowing that he was coming by *later*. Barbara ignored him and began flipping through his CDs to find a song. She found one and pushed play. "Oh, you're just going to ignore me, huh?"

"Yes, because you've always disliked Kurt for no reason." She was wrong, he had a reason. It was because he always occupied her time and Billy didn't like it. But he didn't really know why since she was never *his* girl. Barbara began to sing Rick James and Teena Marie's "Fire and Desire." Billy immediately turned his attention to the back seat of his car and Barbara asked what he was doing.

"Nothing," he said, but he did it again as she continued to sing. He stopped the car before pulling into the driveway because Wilt's putt-putt was in his parking space.

"What are you doing?" she asked. He hopped out of the car, opened her car door, picked her up and carried her like a child as he ran to the back of his house. "Billy put me down, what are you doing?"

"Girl, did you hear that in my car? I'm protecting you."

"Protecting me from what?"

"Your own singing."

She busted out laughing because she knew she was not the greatest singer, but she wasn't as bad as Billy would have her believe.

"Whatever. *I'm not that bad.*" But maybe she should have picked an easier song instead of trying to compete with the vocals of the great Teena Marie. As he put her down, their eyes caught each other, but they quickly turned their attention to Wilt coming outside to the back patio.

"What y'all doing out here?"

"Hey, Wilt."

"Hi, Miss Barbara, you're looking good as usual." He came to give her a genuine hug and then he jumped back. "Damn girl, what's that you're wearing? I need to get Brooke some of that." He took her hand and guided her around so that he could have a closer look.

Billy had seen enough and told Wilt to move his putt-putt out of his parking spot. He then opened the door for Barbara to go inside. Melody was at the door watching the exchange between all three of them. She greeted Barbara and asked her salad dressing preference. Italian was her favorite, but she told Melody to use whatever she had. She made Barbara some collard greens and Yams, along with corn on the cob, and the salad. She'd made her famous meatloaf with gravy, cabbage, green beans, and cornbread for Billy and Wilt. She decided to eat what Barbara ate so she didn't feel left out.

Dinner was over and the mingling led into a game of pool. Billy and Wilt couldn't help making bets with their never-ending competition. So they made a bet that Barbara could beat Wilt. The only problem was, she couldn't beat Wilt because she had never played a game of pool.

"Guys, y'all are going too far. I don't know how to play."

"Okay. I bet you five hundred dollars that Barbara can make this eight ball into the corner pocket," Billy called out.

"Billy, no. I can't. I don't even know how to grip the pool stick." He ignored her and said she could do it and he would teach her. First, he gave her a pool stick and showed her how to put chalk on it. He guided her to the pool table, then taught her how to measure the two balls. He leaned her over the table and showed her how to grip the pool stick with him directly behind her in the same position. She was nervous because she knew that if she missed it, he would owe Wilt *five hundred dollars*. She didn't want to be the reason he lost the bet.

"Billy, I can't do it," she kept exclaiming to him. She didn't want to lose his money even though he would soon be a millionaire with his rookie contract.

"It's okay. Just focus. You can do it." He kept reassuring her. Her nerves began to get the best of her. It was all too much with Melody and Wilt watching and Billy against her backside helping her line up the shot. He whispered in her ear. "You got this. Wilt owes me." He placed his hand softly on top of hers and explained how to line the stick up and gently hit the ball based on the distance it needed to travel and the speed it would take to get there. Wilt continued to talk, and Melody told him to let her concentrate. She cheered Barbara on, saying that she could do it. The room went quiet, and everything appeared to be in slow motion as Barbara watched the white ball hit the black eight ball, it stopped at the edge of the corner pocket, and dropped in. Billy and Melody cheered as he high-fived Barbara and told her he knew she could do it.

Billy walked over to Wilt and held out his hand. Wilt said, "Double or nothing." As soon as he said that, his cell phone rang, and it was Brooke. She needed him before her friend's wedding tomorrow.

"Look, I'm going to have to go to the ATM. I'll get you your money tomorrow."

"Wilt, why you lyin'? I will charge it to your long overdue tab."

"Whatever man, peace out. Thanks for the dinner, Mrs. Daye, and Miss Barbara, see your *beautiful self* soon."

Billy gave him a look that seemed to say, *Get yo' ass out of my house with that playboy mentality **and** you owe me five hundred dollars.* Wilt started laughing because he knew exactly what Billy was thinking. It was the same look he always got when Wilt flirted with *Barbara*. Billy walked Wilt to the front door and watched him skedaddle down the street. He locked the door and went back into the game room to join his mother and Barbara.

Melody asked if he or Barbara needed anything because she was going to call it a night. Billy and Barbara wished her a good night and said they were going to play a few more games of pool before he took Barbara home.

"All right. Barbara, it was fun company. You need to come by more often, even when Billy leaves for camp next week."

Barbara was taken aback because she knew he was leaving but hadn't known it would be this soon. What was she going to do without him? Billy gestured for his mom to be quiet because he hadn't told Barbara his plans yet. He noticed the saddened look on her face, and it didn't sit well with him. He tried to change the vibe by giving her further lessons on how to play pool. She watched and listened like it was the Gospel. He methodically emphasized each movement and took her in his arms to continue to demonstrate. He was ecstatic about how fast she was learning.

"There you go, Barbara. You're getting it."

She was so happy and so was he. Their eyes met like deer caught in headlights. She tried to turn away, but she couldn't, and neither could he. The pent-up emotions between the two of them were beginning to heat up like boiling water. And neither knew how to stop it. Billy took the pool stick from her hand and placed it against the table. She shifted so her backside touched the table with him directly in front of her, and then it happened. He took his hands and cupped the back of her head, pulling her close to him, and gently kissed her. He waited for her cue on whether to continue, and finally she leaned into him and reciprocated. The kiss lasted way too long for friends, but was way too short for lovers.

"So, when were you going to tell me that you were leaving next week?" He sighed and said he had been waiting for the perfect time. "But soon." He apologized that she had to hear it from his mother first. She tried to lower her head but he lifted it, looking directly into her eyes. "Barbara, I'm sorry. The last thing I want to do is hurt you."

A tear fell from her eyes and he wiped it.

"I'm going to always be here for you. Always." He took her into his arms and held her tight. She wanted to stay there forever, and he wanted the same. He lifted her chin with his forefinger, and they kissed as long as lovers this time, then he picked her up and carried her to his bedroom. She never took her eyes off him as they disrobed and made love for the very first time. When it was over, she felt embarrassed because it had gone against her principles of marriage before sex. They both got dressed and she asked that he take her home *immediately,* and he did. The ride to her house was very different. It was loaded with immoral feelings, guilt, and trepidation. What would become of their friendship now that they had crossed the line?

Her house was dark, and he offered to walk her inside, but she refused. She could no longer look at him. Even though she refused, he still got out of the car and walked her to the door. She fumbled with her key until he took it out of her hand and unlocked the door. He apologized profusely, but she wasn't trying to hear it. They'd had sex less than four months after her fiancé's death, and he was her cousin's ex-boyfriend.

"Barbara, are you going to talk to me? Please don't do this." She said nothing but continued inside and closed the door behind her. She went into her room and cried. She sobbed and asked God for forgiveness. She didn't know why or how it happened, but she had given her virginity to Billy Daye, and there was nothing she could do to take it back.

Chapter Twenty-One

Barbara was still in disbelief over what she and Billy had done the night before as she waited impatiently at a restaurant for her mother to arrive. Billy constantly calling and texting her for forgiveness only made matters worse, so she tried to block him out of her mind, and in doing so removed him from her contact list. She was trying to focus on her mother and why she was running late. She knew her mother desperately needed her and didn't want any distractions. Besides, Billy was leaving town next week and she felt it was better not to see him before he left.

Jenny walked into the restaurant looking paranoid and homely with a headwrap that didn't match her attire. Barbara waved her over to the back table. Jenny noticed her but didn't even crack a smile of endearment. Barbara stood up to greet her mother with a hug. Jenny held her tight, and Barbara knew something was wrong. They sat down across from each other.

"Hey, Mama, how are you? Did you come alone? Where's Hakeem?" She kept rambling off questions because she wanted to get straight to the point and find out why she wanted to meet so urgently.

"Barbara, Hakeem and I are no longer together, and I've been living in a shelter."

"What? Mama, why didn't you call me sooner and let me know? I mean, can't you just move back home with Grandma?"

"I didn't call because you had your own heartache with your fiancé passing and I didn't want to burden you. As far as my mother, I can't have that woman trying to run my life. But that's not what I'm here to talk about."

Her hands were shaking like someone who didn't like public speaking. Then she began to tell Barbara how she went to her yearly mammogram appointment, and they found a lump in her left breast. The doctors performed a biopsy and found that the lump was cancerous. She had been taking chemotherapy and was getting weaker by the day. Jenny began to tear up telling her about the treatments and how they were affecting her. Barbara stood up and sat next to her mother to comfort her and let her know she believed in The Most High and that He had the final word. Jenny began to cry even harder when she told Barbara that Hakeem had left her as soon as he found out she had cancer. Barbara didn't know what to do or say. She had to get back to work on Monday morning. Her students needed her and so did her mother. She thought about asking her father if Jenny could temporarily move in with them.

"Mama, would you mind if I ask Dad to let you stay with us until your cancer is gone?"

"You know how Leon feels about me for ruining Christmas. I don't think that's a good idea—"

Barbara stopped her mid-sentence because she couldn't and wouldn't have her mother living at a shelter, especially needing medical attention. Barbara thought about putting her mother into a hotel until she figured out a permanent residence. They talked about the temporary living arrangement and Jenny agreed to it. They ordered their meals, and each ate very little before they left to find a hotel room. Barbara paid for three months and promised her mother that she would check on her often. She went by Walmart to buy groceries, and soon after left her mother in a nice, safe environment with plenty of food.

When she arrived home, Billy was parked in front of the house. She let out a sigh because it was not the time to be dealing with him. He got out of the car as soon as he saw her pull into the driveway. She tried to hurry into the house, but his rapid stride was too much for her.

"Barbara, let me talk to you," he pleaded.

"Talk about what? That you're leaving next week, huh? Well, I already know."

"No, talk about *us* and what happened last night. Why are you giving me the third-degree silent treatment?"

Reliving the previous night and the memory of the encounter made her break down. She told him how she broke her promise to The Most High to stay a virgin until marriage, that he'd taken that all away, and now she was being punished because her mother had breast cancer.

"Now, go away Billy Daye, and leave me alone. Go on with your life *and* there is no *us*."

She walked inside the house, locked the door, and slid to the floor crying. Billy could hear her and begged her to open the door, but she wouldn't. Her emotions over him and her mother had taken their toll. She had to get herself together for work the next day. Billy waited another five minutes before leaving. He sped away and felt so stupid for hurting his best friend, the woman who he adored as much as his mother.

Leon arrived home shortly after Barbara but noticed after several hours that she still hadn't come out of her room. He had been waiting for her to come and talk to him about her meeting with Jenny.

He noticed his daily newspaper missing and wondered if they hadn't delivered it yet. He gently tapped on Barbara's bedroom door in case she was asleep but she wasn't. She sat in her bed looking for an apartment for her mother.

"Come in," she answered. Leon walked in and noticed his newspaper spread across her bed with red circles drawn around specific sections. She was old school and still used the paper.

"Hey, Pumpkin, did I catch you at a bad time? Is everything all right?" The look on her face told him that she had been crying.

"Oh, Daddy." She began to cry like a child, telling him about Jenny and ending her conversation with Billy leaving the next week. Leon didn't know where to start so he began with Jenny and offered to help pay for her apartment. He volunteered to take her to appointments and help as much as possible. He wasn't a fan of Jenny, but he was willing to put their differences aside for the greater good if that would win his daughter's happiness.

He then tackled what could be his daughter's greatest heartache, and that was Billy moving to Washington, DC. He explained to her that he had no choice because that was how the NFL was structured. "I know he didn't want to leave you, and maybe he didn't know when or how to tell you that he was leaving so soon. I can't fault him for wanting to protect you."

But that was only part of Barbara's tears. The other half was her broken promise about losing her virginity. Leon continued to comfort her, to let her know that it was going to be all right, and Billy was a great guy. It was normal for women to act in a different way than men after their first-time having sex.

"Dad, why do I feel like I hate Billy?"

"Because you don't. In fact, I think he's your first true love."

Barbara began to sob even more because she felt her dad was right, even though she wanted him to be wrong. But Billy was going to be an NFL star with a gazillion women throwing themselves at him. Not to mention the fact that he was handsome with a genuine heart. She was afraid to compete and her only option was to push him away.

Chapter Twenty-Two

Barbara walked into her classroom to prepare for the students before they returned from Christmas break. She had just come from her mother's apartment where she was happy to hear that her cancer was in remission. She no longer wore the headwrap because her hair had fully grown back, she'd gained weight, and was ready to look for a job. Her father kept his promise and had helped her get back on her feet. She was happy that they had buried their resentment and were better friends than when they were together.

It had been a long eight months attending to her own health, and her mother's, and she was looking forward to a leave of absence that she desperately needed. Her feet were tired, and she could barely see them due to her growing belly. She had begun to see the doctor weekly due to her elevated blood pressure. Her plan for that day was to stop by her classroom and then go in to see Dr. Suarez. She left after an hour and was on her way downtown to the doctor's office when she decided to get a bite to eat before checking in with the nurse's assistant. While she was downstairs in the lobby, she ran into Melody.

"Barbara Knight. Is that you?" Melody asked because she wasn't quite sure. Barbara had put on weight, straightened her hair, and wore a chignon with bangs.

"Hi, Mrs. Daye. Yes, it's me."

"How are you? It's so good to see you. I haven't seen you since Billy left eight months ago." She stepped back to take in Barbara's appearance and couldn't help but notice her growing belly. She rubbed Barbara's stomach and asked about her due date. Barbara took her finger and pulled back an imaginary piece of hair that wasn't out of place, tucking it behind her ear due to nerves.

"Oh, I'm actually due in another three weeks, but my doctor thinks the baby will come a lot sooner."

"I have to mention to Billy that I saw you and that you are expecting a baby."

"Um, Mrs. Daye, can you please not mention it to Billy?"

"Well, if you insist. You know he could be a little jealous of the father-to-be because he has always had a crush on you."

They talked for another ten minutes, and Melody told Barbara not to be a stranger. She even said she was available to take care of her unborn child since she was only working part-time at the hospital. Barbara promised that she would keep in touch and even stored her number in her contact list. Melody hugged her and told her to take care of herself, and if she needed anything to call.

Billy Daye had taken the NFL by storm, a young handsome rookie from San Antonio, Texas who held the passing and rushing yard rookie record, surpassing the Atlanta Falcons', Michael Vick and Payton Manning of the Denver Broncos. He was on the cover of every magazine from *The Source* to *Sports Illustrated* and deemed one of the most handsome eligible bachelors.

You couldn't turn on the TV without a commercial endorsing or sponsoring Billy Daye.

Grown men wanted to be him and the women wanted to be with him. He was in Washington living his best life alongside his agent, Wilt Jackson.

"Man, how many more interviews do I have to give?" Billy asked Wilt. He was fortunate that Brooke hadn't been pregnant, and he had Wilt as his agent, but felt Wilt was scheduling too many interviews and endorsement deals. Wilt had become a top-notch sought-after agent after acquiring Billy, a lucrative rookie contract worth twenty-five million for four years and all of it guaranteed.

"Did you order the car for my sister and Mrs. Wilson?" Billy had made a pact with his teacher in high school that when he made it to the NFL he would hook her up, and he made sure his family was taken care of as well. Except his mother didn't want a new house or car, so Billy opened her a Roth IRA account and maxed it out. He also bought Wilt a new car of his choice as a sign-on bonus for being his agent.

"Yes, I took care of all that. The cars should be delivered by tomorrow afternoon." Billy gave Wilt full access to all his financials, and Wilt handled all his business professionally and with proficiency.

The Washington Redskins were heading to the playoffs for the first time in ten years with Billy at the helm. His superstardom was growing at the speed of light and he hadn't been back home since he left for camp. His mom and sister came to visit him last month when he played against the Dallas Cowboys on Thanksgiving Day. Brandy had a seat in the box level, but his mother stayed at the condo that he shared with Wilt. She still couldn't watch him play such a violent game. Her only request was a phone call to let her know her son was safe.

He thought about Barbara from time to time, but he had put her out of his mind because he needed to focus on the game he loved. After a few months of calling and not getting an answer, he moved on and became a megastar. But to his family, he was just Billy. A brother and a son, as well as a good friend.

Billy pulled out the playbook and began watching the Atlanta Falcons' game video. Washington would play them in the first round of the playoffs. He watched Vick's feet and how quick and fast he was, and the tough Falcons defense. He knew he had his work cut out for him. He nursed his sore shoulder but never took his eyes from the video. After chatting with Wilt, he departed, and most of his time was spent studying game film.

Leon ordered a veggie pizza and wings, and sat down to watch the first playoff game, the Redskins and the Falcons. He wore a Billy Daye number 2 jersey. Barbara and Jenny entered a short time later after doing a little shopping for the baby. Leon helped with all the bags and took them to the extra room that was made into a nursery for his grandchild.

"Uh, we tried to get back as fast as we could before the game started," Barbara said. "Well, it's about ten minutes until kickoff."

Jenny took a pillow to prop her daughter's back and helped place her feet on the ottoman.

Billy was plastered all over the television, and as he was on the field warming up, one of the reporters began interviewing him about his stats and the article in *Sports Illustrated* about him being one of the most eligible bachelors.

"Billy Daye, can I please have a word with you?" she asked as she held her microphone about an inch away from his mouth.

"Sure."

"What do you feel that you need to do against Michael Vick and the Atlanta Falcons to win?"

"I just need to focus on the game plan and the rest will take care of itself. Coach has prepared us well and we will see if we can execute."

"What do you think about Michael Vick and stopping his dual attack of running and passing ability?"

"I mean, Mike is a beast. He's Super Mike, and there's no way we can stop him. Our defense can only hope to contain him."

"Billy, one more question. There's an article about you being an eligible bachelor. You don't have a special someone in your life, do you?" Billy was taken aback by the last question and looked directly into the camera.

"That's right. I'm a single man, ladies." He did his signature eye wink and ran into the locker room to get ready for the Atlanta Falcons.

Barbara's heart nearly stopped because Billy's eye wink had always been a silent killer. But the fact that he was letting America know he was eligible was the reason she had decided not to answer or return his calls. She refused to be in competition. She wanted him to focus on his career and she didn't want to be a distraction. Leon and Jenny watched Barbara's reaction after Billy's interview and knew that it had affected her. There she sat, unmarried, carrying his unborn child. Leon cleared his throat in an effort to distract Barbara and asked if anyone wanted pizza. Both Jenny and Barbara were famished. They ate and watched Billy win his first playoff game with a score of 21 to 20.

The day had been cold, but Barbara welcomed it. She was on her three-month maternity leave and was in the last week before her expected due date. She could hardly wait until it was all over. Each night before going to bed she would read and play classical music to her unborn child. She wanted to keep the sex a surprise, so she decorated the nursery in unisex blue and yellow. She placed articles about Billy inside her scrapbook and would read them to her belly, saying, "Let's read about your father." She held a full conversation, and like clockwork, the baby turned somersaults with just the mention of Billy's name.

Jenny asked if she could come in and talk to Barbara. Leon was going to drop her off at her apartment, so she wanted to check on her before she left. Jenny didn't mince words and cut straight to it.

"You know you can't keep this a secret forever, right? Billy is going to find out, especially after seeing his mother a few weeks ago. He's going to know, Barbara. And besides, he's the father. It's his right to know."

Before Barbara could answer she felt a hard kick to her stomach followed by a cramp. She grabbed her belly and breathed in and out because it took her breath away.

"Barbara, are you okay?"

Barbara couldn't speak, so Jenny called Leon, and within minutes he had her in the car and they were headed to Methodist Hospital. When they arrived Barbara's contractions were twenty minutes apart. The nurse guided her to a room where they administered an IV, took her vitals, and began giving her an enema.

Leon paced back and forth, trying to decide if he should call Melody and tell her to contact Billy so he could get there quickly. But he didn't have to call because Melody was the nurse assigned to attend to Barbara. After the anesthesiologist administered an epidural Barbara fell fast asleep. Jenny told Melody that Barbara was having her grandchild and Billy was the father. Melody couldn't believe her ears. She immediately contacted Billy to tell him he needed to get to Methodist Hospital and fast. She mentioned Barbara and a baby, and told him not to ask any questions, just get there as fast as he could. Thankfully, Billy was in Dallas to take on the Cowboys that Sunday, so he wasn't far away.

Jenny contacted Lizzy and Sasha to let them know that Barbara was in labor and it was time for her to have her baby.

Billy and Wilt arrived at the airport not knowing what they were there for. All they knew was that it had something to do with Barbara and a baby.

"Man, did you sleep with Barbara before you left town?"

Billy ignored Wilt because when it came to Barbara there was no kiss and tell.

"You told me to cover my stick and you got your 'friend' pregnant? Man, I can't believe you. I just hope that baby doesn't come out looking like you." Wilt joked to try and lighten the mood.

"Wilt, can you please let me think? I don't know what's going on. Why you jumpin' to conclusions?" Wilt continued saying that he wasn't jumpin' to anything. He knew Billy was in love with Barbara because he hadn't slept with anybody in months, and now he was breaking his neck to get back to San Antonio for her.

When Billy and Wilt arrived, they went to the nurse's station to ask for Barbara Knight, but only the immediate family was allowed information when it came to her condition. Sasha saw Billy and Wilt and called them over, letting the nurse know that he was family.

"Sasha, what's going on? Where is Barbara?"

"She's in Room 210." Sasha pointed, standing hand-in-hand with Rashad. Billy and Wilt walked into the room and saw Barbara asleep. Her belly was huge.

"Mama, what's going on?" Billy asked as he continued looking at Barbara and her stomach.

"Billy, Barbara is pregnant with your child."

"What? Mama, why didn't someone tell me? I can't believe this," Billy continued. "No, I can't let my baby come into this world without being married. I know how Barbara feels about it too." Barbara heard Billy's voice, but thought she was dreaming. She was groggy from the epidural.

"Billy, is that you?"

"Barbara, yes, it's me. I'm here. why didn't you call and tell me you were pregnant?" He kept grabbing his head in disbelief. He wanted answers.

"I wanted you to stay focused on your football." He cut her off and told her he didn't care about football and that she and his unborn child meant everything to him. He then grabbed her hand and said the baby couldn't be born without a father. He was there to handle his responsibilities as a man. He felt bad about her broken promise to God. He needed to make it right.

"Barbara, please marry me. Leon, can I have your daughter's hand in marriage? Please?" His emotions were all over the place.

Leon grabbed Billy and pulled him into his arms, giving him his well wishes. Jimmy sat there and thought Billy should be asking him, but it wasn't the time or place, so he stayed quiet next to Lizzy.

"Marry you? What? When?"

"Right now, before the baby is born. Barbara, will you marry me right now?"

She nodded her head, then thought about it for a second.

"But do you love me?" She wanted to make sure he was marrying her for love and not because of the baby.

"I can answer that for you, Barbara. The man is crazy about you. He ain't had no pus—" Wilt blurted, but Melody cut him off from using that vulgar language.

Billy didn't object and said he had been in love with her since high school, but he was too afraid to admit it. Sasha rolled her eyes thinking, *I knew it.*

"Is that a yes?"

"Yes, Billy, I will marry you."

Billy asked Wilt to go get an ordained minister. Wilt ran out of the room and asked the nurse, explaining that his friend needed to get married before his baby was born. She said that she would send Rev. Hurd into the room.

When Wilt got back, Brandy had arrived and was standing next to her brother, holding him. She couldn't believe she was going to be an auntie. Wilt said the minister would be in soon to perform the nuptials.

Five minutes later, Kurt walked into the room holding a bible. Billy was about to lose his cool when Barbara grabbed his hand.

"Man, what are you doing here?"

"I was called because someone needed a minister?"

Barbara had forgotten that Kurt not only had his plumbing business, but he was also an ordained minister. Billy couldn't believe it, and time was ticking, so he obliged and let Kurt do the nuptials. Kurt wasn't happy either, but he put his feelings aside because he was doing what God had called him to do, and that was to perform vows under His word.

Kurt began: "Bill Daye, do you take Miss Barbara Knight to be your lawfully wedded wife?"

"That's *Billy,* and yes, I take Barbara to be my life. I mean, wife." He was so nervous because Barbara's contractions were starting up again and she'd begun grunting in pain.

She sped it up and shouted, "Yes, I do." even before Kurt asked her.

Billy didn't have a ring and said he would make it up to her, but then Wilt tapped his shoulder and gave him a small box. He opened it and there was a four-carat solitaire ring with a matching wedding band. He nodded to Wilt thinking, *that's my man. Always coming through when I need him.* Billy took the rings, placed them on Barbara's ring finger, and kissed her passionately. Kurt hadn't even gotten to the *kiss your bride* part.

"See, that's what got y'all here in the first place," Brandy shouted. Everyone erupted in laughter as Kurt pronounced them husband and wife. Mr. and Mrs. Billy Daye tied the knot before their child was born.

Barbara was wheeled into the delivery room with Billy, Jenny, and Leon by her side. Billy came out fifteen minutes later to let everyone know that he was a father and Barbara was recovering well. After hearing the news, they all went down to the cafeteria to get a bite to eat and waited until Barbara was back in her room. Mrs. Rosenthal, the representative for vital records came in to get information from Barbara and wanted to know the name of the child. Barbara asked that she return shortly because the father had gone to get something to eat. She didn't want to name the baby without him.

Within minutes everyone had gathered in Barbara's room, and they were waiting for the nurse to bring the baby from the nursery.

The baby arrived and everyone coddled her and said how much she looked like Billy.

"Aww damn, poor baby. I was hoping she'd look more like her mother," Wilt called out.

"Wilt, be quiet." Brandy chuckled, saying that her brother was handsome.

Billy was all over Barbara. He even asked her to scoot over so he could lay next to her. She told him that Mrs. Rosenthal was waiting for a name and would be back soon.

Mrs. Rosenthal walked in and asked Barbara for a name. Barbara introduced Billy Daye as her husband and father of her child. "Oh yes, Mr. Daye, the football star. Do you have a name for your daughter?"

Billy walked over to the small crib where she slept snuggled in her blanket. He picked her up, cradling her with both hands, and couldn't believe that she was his.

"Look at her, Mama. We look just like her."

"Yes, son, she looks like us, not we look like her."

"She is beautiful, Mama. Daddy would be so proud."

Barbara whispered to Billy that she needed a name, and that Mrs. Rosenthal was waiting, but Billy was in a trance. He continued admiring his daughter until a tear fell from his eye.

"She reminds me of you, Barbara, everything about her is you." He turned to his wife. "I mean, she's everything to me, just like you are." He continued talking to Barbara about the baby and she nodded her head with tears in her eyes.

"You have made me the happiest man in the world."

"Billy, would you give the baby a name so this woman can go on with her day?" Brandy hissed.

Melody gave her a look that said "cool it."

"I still can't believe it," Billy continued. "Look at how blessed I am. My daughter is going to be a trendsetter," he said. "Barbara, baby, she's going to change the world. You wait and see. She's gorgeous, phenomenal, and she's *my* daughter. I mean, look at her, she's just like her mother...*brilliant*."

Billy looked up with shining eyes.

"She is...Brilliant Daye."

Thank you for reading Brilliant Daye Book 1. I hope you enjoyed it.